Also by Olympia Vernon

Eden

Logic

OLYMPIA VERNON

A KILLING IN THIS TOWN

Grove Press
New York

Published simultaneously in Canada
Printed in the United States of America

FIRST PAPERBACK EDITION

Library of Congress Cataloging-in-Publication Data

Vernon, Olympia.
    A killing in this town / Olympia Vernon.—1st ed.
        p. cm.
    ISBN 0-8021-4296-6
    ISBN 978-0-8021-4296-2
    1. Factories—Safety measures—Fiction. 2. Ku Klux Klan (1915-)—
Fiction. 3. Working class—Fiction. 4. Mississippi—Fiction. 5. Lynching—
Fiction. 6. Racism—Fiction. 7. Boys—Fiction. I. Title.

PS3622.E75K55 2006
813'.6—dc22   2005052547

Grove Press
an imprint of Grove/Atlantic, Inc.
841 Broadway
New York, NY 10003

07 08 09 10   10 9 8 7 6 5 4 3 2 1

There he

—Mose Wright

prologue

And whosoever shall fall on this stone
shall be broken: but on whomsoever
it shall fall, it will grind him to
powder.

Matthew 21:44

chapter one

Earl Thomas was a dead nigger.

And he well knew it.

There was a pulsating rod beneath the muscle in his face where Hoover Pickens had pinned him down at the Pauer Plant nearly thirteen years ago and bade him beg for mercy.

Earl Thomas had only come to deliver the letter: it had come on such a morning when the sun was hungry for attention and soaked his clothes all wet and took to his body—a suffocating moan emerged—the numbers smeared, written in a sudden rebelliousness that leaped from the hand that wrote it.

The night before, a tiny bird landed on the maple. Perhaps it had come from up north where the cold was so still and caught in the blade of its feather that only the atmosphere of a small town could bring it to stay.

Emma New heard no sound at all in the world. Thirty years they'd been married and still the sounds of earth and sky could not bring her to wake when it seemed she was already so safe in her sleeping.

Earl Thomas emerged from the warmth that had become a part of his body, the source of his thinking rising upward, away from the bone. He sat there a moment on the bed's edge and reached through the darkness of the room, as if to balance his hand on the slate of air around him.

A cough erupted. He brought his hand up to his throat and pressed with his large fingers: the cough lay trapped in the distinctive measurement of his larynx.

With his fingertip, he killed it.

The cough was no longer alive but had gone down, back inside his lungs, where he knew it would rise again.

He did not want to wake Emma New.

He turned to where her face was, ungreedy for his hand or love. And now he noticed it: the moon had struck her face with a permanent, solitary stadium of peace and clung to her breathing, as if a match had been lit in the room.

His hand rose over her nostrils, and if ever heaven existed, it was now, when God had seen the possibility and manner of what breathing could predict.

Perhaps it was, indeed, the bird that woke him.

Or this, the moment he realized that love could live in this world and the one after it, if he took to it now, while it breathed in his full mind and body.

This noise, this room, absorbed him, shook him from his place. A cry, unlike the cough in his throat, could not be muzzled: his lips began to tremble.

The trembling was massive. Emma New began to stir: in her momentary waking, she lifted her wrist from her side—a prediction—and whispered quietly: Earl, what's the matter?

He let go of the full cry, the trembling. Thus it came, the beginning words: I just now seen it, Emma New.

He paused. Just now.

She, too, could hear the bird on the maple, and her response told of the matter that she'd woken up to: Come to bed.

But he couldn't come to bed, not now, when he had carried the letter in his pocket for such a long time, held a horrible secret within him that stuck to his ribs. He was good and wholesome in his mindful territory, he could try again and Hoover Pickens would take it and he'd tell Hoover Pickens how he'd tried to give it to him, even if, even if Hoover Pickens called him a nigger.

Tomorrow. Tomorrow. There were no tomorrows in the world of Earl Thomas. Not anymore. It was too late. The government had sent the letter: *To the Men of the Pauer Plant*, it read. *Courtesy of the Pastor*.

Of all the arrangements in the world, this was his, forged into completion: God, too, had sent it to him and only him to tell it, to spread the word to Hoover Pickens and the rest of the Klansmen at the Pauer Plant: Get out of there, he'd say. Run, before your lungs burst.

There were no other pastors in this town. He seemed at once frail and inconsistent, unattached to the thing he possessed, and yet he had sprung forth out of duty to God, to the public: whatever it was that rumbled so, it took him, drove him into the ground and earth with it.

He'd heard what they'd done to niggers, how they'd dragged the bodies out, turned them on the face. He heard it in his mind, the bones ground into powder, until a cloud—the dust of vertebrae—rose in the hot wind, the torrential predicament of a bloody thunderhead.

Hoover Pickens had pinned him down, called him a nigger: the image of what he looked like, they, the men, how they looked down on him, tossed him about on the ground, his face swelling in the dust. He had begged, called out: God, he whispered. God.

Earl Thomas had drawn a line.

No matter who had sent him to tell it, he somehow felt esteemed, privileged.

And yet he could not sleep. He was contradictory.

He turned toward Emma New: her stomach had begun to churn.

He was no longer safe there. Noise and regret in the same room at the same time, unfascinating and disobedient, could not live in his head and be free.

He lifted himself from the bed.

He thought of the widow: Sonny had lost her husband.

Dragged to death.

Sonny and Curtis Willow lived on the other side of the forest: the happening was so quick and sedative in his mind that he wanted to vomit. A boy had called Curtis from the house, Sonny behind him in a gown that smothered her weight. They took him, Hoover Pickens and the others, the white men on their horses, and hitched him up to a pulley, dragged him, until his face burned at the root, his lower mandible detached, until his torso snapped.

They said he lost an eye.

The sound of shock and wailing, the sound of hate and body—both together—were so heavy in Earl Thomas's mind that they reached inward, where his gut was, and shook the transparency of the thing he had kept, a dangling stone.

He hoped that the letter could've ended the hatred of the Bullock, Mississippi, Klansmen: the alphabets of the letter were so beautifully aligned, the scent of the sweated and dried-out ink could've filled the Pauer Plant and the men—they could've gotten out of there, gone home to where a man should've been when danger was unsuitable for living.

If only they knew.

But the other words, the other alphabets, loud and dirty in his mind they were, at once, altogether bellowing out: Nigger. Nigger, you're dead.

The boy, he thought of him now.

It was a ritual in the town of Bullock, Mississippi. On the eve of a boy's manhood, thirteen, he must become a member. He must go out to a nigger's house and call him out of it. He's got to tell the others, abed his horse, to hitch the nigger up to the pulley, hands tied. Feet tied. And drag him, drag the nigger through the woods, until his torso is bloody and his head and body are bloody.

Until he loses an eye.

Hoover Pickens's boy, Adam, was now coming of age.

He'd have to find him a nigger to drag.

Earl Thomas thought of this, before the bird had become so full of the world and its odor that it flew into the mouth of the moon, where it seemed the face of Emma New Thomas had gone back to sleep.

chapter
two

Hoover Pickens's lungs hurt.

He stood out on the breakfast porch: his breathing had begun to slow down in the morning time, as it had at night, when the fascinating detail of a flying insect both woke and stirred him to whisper.

He simply could not sleep.

Something uncontrollable, bloody, was in his lungs. Whether it was the rummaging noise of a mosquito, blind to the truth within him, or the slow murmur of age that crept into his breathing eardrum, he could not find it lying down. And, upon occasion, emerged from his slumber with a humbling of the bones that denied him evolution.

He had grown into a tired, systematic dream of his own doing. He never woke from it: he had gone down to a wooded and full tree and looked upward to where the sun had received no apology from his living and hateful body; it moved farther away in the distance, as if it was embarrassment that provoked its mobility.

He whispered into the wooded tree, whispered and could not remember what brought it out of his lungs, and could not, for the coldness of his nature, hear it. Although it had come from him, was born and sprung forth from his heart, the eardrum was the organ that would not accept it.

A cold and dirty sweat awaited him. He shook in his clothes and waited for the whisper and the dream both to deliver their message to the hot summer wind, so that he could forget he'd ever lived it.

The whisper was not born of apology or any such thing. It was without face or eye: it was malicious and fell down upon him with an odor that rushed throughout his bloody lung and quit.

The missis had laid his plate on a small, rotted table on the breakfast porch, but he was not hungry this morning.

He walked away from the house and into the yard of dust around him. He looked down at his shoe where his foot was and wanted to move the ground from beneath him. God had made it so.

For he felt a man ought to be able to move his foot and shake the earth around him, especially when this part was his. He was a part of his own thinking this morning, but there was never a line in his head that offered regret.

There was none.

No lines of regret for Sonny or Curtis. When he thought of Sonny Willow, a laughter rose within him and he spat on the ground, as if to say: Here's your Curtis.

He remembered the look of terrifying exhaustion in her cheek, and it was well with him that they had put it there: they had caused a frightening detail to rise in her face, saw her there in the gown that mocked her weight, how lonesome she was when he tied Curtis down to the pulley.

He laughed now: the sun, as it had in his dreams, found its mobility. He looked up at the oracle above him and shook his fist at it.

He had begun to sweat in his shoe.

D. D. Pickens appeared through the screen door and, in her wisdom, walked out onto the breakfast porch where she called him to live.

Hoover Pickens, you ain't worth a soul hungry, she yelled.

He turned to face her. Her body had become pitiful: the face was brittle, a hint of mockingbird bone. The breasts beneath the gown that shattered any possibility of want. Her beauty had come early in the world, when he stood behind her at the window and put a seed in her belly.

In a minute, D.D., he whispered.

She turned, her face against the bed of the screen, and sighed.

She did not know it, but her face was a disease: it was so sick in Hoover Pickens's mind that he plucked it from her standing place and threw it down there where the dust could make it even with the world.

She was dirty.

She did not at all exist.

A long year had made it that way: the pregnancy, late and full-blown, caused an agony in her foot that took its course up her calf and there fell, the pain of her vagina, life coming out.

Hoover Pickens was unremorseful. It was her complaining, the constant moaning of the fever. How he wanted her to hush. Her body was made for this: a woman, in his ripe and full eye, was made to burst.

She was to take it, the pain and fever and the agonizing foot, the pain of her vagina. The hurt. He hated her at that particular moment, for the yelling of the matter. It was his, the boy was his, and she was to push it out without complaint.

She was to take it like a man took it when he called a nigger from his house and dragged him. He saw her there, pushing and weaving herself into a falsetto, and it was the doctor who stopped him from pulling the boy out: Adam, his son, had come.

Hoover Pickens looked up from the dust of his foot.

Midnight, the mutt, disturbed his memory. He had lived as long as Adam. Adam had been born sick and weak at birth: D. D. Pickens reached for her hat, went into town near the Feed and Seed store, and cradled Midnight in her arms. It was customary: the dog had to breathe this child's air, live with him until the sickness had passed into his own body. It was the vitamins of the tongue that saved, shifted the bad blood out of the boy, until it slept, without ease, in Midnight's own body and came out in his feces.

Midnight had given Adam life: he had breathed it all in, the sickness and the heart of this child he had come to love with an immeasurable tribe of energy.

Midnight now lay on the breakfast porch.

Adam had not yet come down this morning, but soon he would emerge from the steps of this house and through the screen door to where his father, with his irregular and painful lungs, had now disappeared into the mouth of the adjacent barn.

chapter three

It was evening time.

Earl Thomas had come out of his house. He paused for a moment in his position: the sky was unusually orange now, a bit of honeysuckle floating in the air around him.

He lifted his hand. The scene of the sun going down over the town permeated the space between his fingers and traveled down his neck. The orange hue of its dictatorship covered his bones.

He closed his eyes. The warmth of the universe swelled inside his mouth. He took what the air had given him. He had a sermon to prepare for tomorrow and he'd tell it to the church like he told it to God: My spirit, it's dead.

The breathing in his face came to a halt.

He heard it, just on the other side of the woods, the loud and bitter voices coming from the Pickens house. The Klan was having a meeting tonight. They were out near the barn and they were stepping down from their horses and . . . it was the laughter he heard through the trees. The laughter that fell down upon him, the laughter he'd heard all these years that made him hold the letter.

If Sonny'd just hold on now.

If she'd just . . . The warmth had left him, the sun fully hidden from the eye.

Suddenly, a muscle lifted the vein in his face and pounded, pounded as if it had heard this. The tip of his finger had begun to press down on the muscle, as if by controlling it, the sound of the laughter would disappear.

But nothing could stop it now.

It burst out of him, the sound and echo of his prayer.

He realized now: the honeysuckle was dead.

The laughter heard by Earl Thomas had come from the Klansmen.

They were describing the torso of Curtis Willow: all swollen and rotted at the root. The muscles restricted, the jawbone open and wide. A tiny caterpillar had crept into his mouth at death and clung to the bones of his larynx to the point of a desperate and living place to lie down.

Hoover Pickens coughed.

Factory blood had come out of his lungs tonight, as it had those of Salem and Hurry Bullock, who were on their horses looking down on him. Born of the same womb, the same yellow hair and stained bodies: measured accurately at will, as if by some privileged hope, they ran through this town with a horrible stench of laughter that drew upon their posture the profound slope of malignancy.

Salem and Hurry Bullock had been the factory overseers until Hurry was elected coroner. There leaked within their blood a history of fathers and grandfathers who owned Bullock, Mississippi: the lineage of power.

Salem Bullock leaned heavily on the mane of the horse, his body to one side: his hand had begun to quiver. His wrist lacked elasticity, the bone marrow awakened by a sharp turn of his weight on the arm.

How'd it look? asked Hoover Pickens. Tell us again what it looked like.

The *it* to which he referred was, of course, Curtis Willow.

Merciful, whispered Hurry. Like a kite.

The air grew complex around them, as if they'd all heard the syntax of the darkness creeping into their conversation and stirring, stirring within the creatures that surrounded them.

No one laughed now. They had become disturbed by something. Hoover Pickens noticed the quivering hand of Salem Bullock; the moon, in its grand and stark position, had announced its discomfort.

Someone had to kill it, this frightening position they had found themselves in.

Hurry Bullock laughed, his laughter a hint of devastation.

The others joined him.

No one had thought of it, not now or before: it was underfoot, down near the dust, rising from the earth: an impatient coating of the season. Down, down near the dust and organ that would send them rushing for the throat, the symptoms of suffocating history in their bones.

Yeah, added Salem Pickens, like a kite.

Hurry Bullock saw Adam in the high window of the Pickens house.

Adam rested his hand near the green and withered curtain of his bedroom: he looked at the men below. They were, at once, unfascinating, invisibly perplexed.

He envisioned a river of blood.

His father's face was as unkind and empty as the hate that lived in it.

Now, his hand was out of view, the curtain closed.

That's our hope so high, said Hurry.

Surely, said Hoover Pickens, Not long. Thirteen.

Now Hoover Pickens thought of the days following Earl Thomas's visit to the Pauer Plant, how all the workers had come through the woods, their heads bent low in some uncertain cause, until their laughter halted: the doors of the Pauer Plant had been padlocked.

Boys, said Salem, we done shut down.

It went unseen, the code that drew him and the other factory workers together at the hemming line, drew them near and forced the stitch of ink between their painful and linear bodies.

With thirty years of factory work between them, each man, each in his own fragility, turned to the others and paused. The matter of their uncertainty, the laughter they had only just shared, broke in a marriage of silence, burden.

Hoover Pickens whispered, I'm going home.

Invisibly, he had spoken, too, to Earl Thomas. For it was Earl Thomas who had brought such darkness over the place, such wind and air that it seemed all of them could no longer breathe.

Just then the barn door opened and the horses began to collide with the inexhaustible running of Midnight, who broke with a haunting speed between them and howled.

The horses, in their animal language, began to scatter.

Salem Bullock howled in a tone of rebellion and disappeared through the woods, Hurry trailing behind him where the dust spun Hoover Pickens out of position, bearing the solitary, invisible crux of his vulnerability.

chapter
four

Adam Pickens's face was a rapid and bellowing blaze: his round head carried it for as long as it took. It was his figure that spared him: he was a slow and steady curve, leaning forward into the bone. His vertebrae had begun to tilt.

His yellow hair was singed with drought: he came down the stairs of the house. The wind was pregnant. The unspeakable terrain of the morning had spat him out.

D.D. had found her place near the stove, a large ceramic bowl before her. She spun the wet flour: the silver ladle brought forth the sound of rain.

Adam, she uttered.

He did not respond, but sat still at the kitchen table. He was bewildered by an intolerable noise: a hummingbird had come into the house this early morning. He wondered how it breathed and balanced, how it had acquired some nature about it that lay unconfined and systematic.

D.D. continued to spin the flour, as it would take some greater noise to disturb the matter of her duty. A flying creature, this thing that lived with permanency, rose and hung above her.

Adam spoke, as he had when a line trickled down the side of his ripe eardrum.

Mama, what's the difference between a nigger and a bird?

The silver ladle came to a halt.

I don't know.

A nigger. A bird, whispered Adam. It don't sound right. Even when you say it in your head.

The silver ladle had brought the sound of rain into the house and no one, not even D. D. Pickens, could tame it. The shape, the pattern of its mocking, wove into her face a ravine.

A nigger. A bird, said Adam. I looked it up in the word book. All words. No pictures.

He paused.

D. D. Pickens thought of his birth and how the doctor had pulled him out: she could tell by the positioning of his feet that wisdom was what had brought him into the world.

Midnight came to the door, his head sideways, and flattened his belly on the breakfast porch.

When a bird falls to the ground, asked Adam, where's it go?

D.D. shook her head and had become aware of the wandering hummingbird.

Adam continued, Heaven, Mama? Heaven's where it goes?

That's up to God, she moaned.

I done asked God, said Adam. He never said.

He's busy, son.

What's He busy doin'? Adam asked.

God's got savin' to do, Adam. D.D. continued her stirring, as if the rain hadn't come down equally enough to measure the content of speech and blood in the air and send it crashing down, away from this house and the inquisitive odor around her. D.D. turned and faced Adam, both trapped in the temperature of their hot and varied language: Grace.

But Mama, said Adam. You say grace is when God gives you something you don't deserve.

D.D. was amid the bellowing blaze of Adam: she wished she had never spoken of God in this house, when her vocabulary had grown so lynched in the boy's mind that nothing could bring him down.

Adam, she whispered. You done come through.

Now the memory of her mind and heart fluttered with the pace of the hummingbird: Adam had come from her vagina, like thread through a needle, come into the bursting world wet and with wisdom, and nothing, not even the sound of rain the ladle made, would keep him mute.

You done come through, she repeated, but by this time, Adam had closed the screen door and was lying on the breakfast porch in the precise and paralyzing posture of a blade.

chapter
five

Sonny woke from her bed nude.

Her thumb had begun to pound. She had slept on her belly, her hand beneath her breasts where she had crushed the thumb bone into the remaining territory of her full hand.

A throbbing pain accompanied the movement.

No flexibility.

She seemed a terrifying excursion: Curtis was a blurring relic in this house, a tornado that had come and spun its divinity into the shape of a debilitating dream.

She had only now regained her appetite: her exposed and heavy gut had begun to bring forth a rhythm to her belly. Hunger.

A silent and daring term of forgiveness lay in her dark and golden face. It covered her full head and crowded any expression of pity.

They had come, the white men, as they had roamed in her sleep, to devour, to hate what had not been, ever, the enemy.

They had come to take, to steal her Curtis from his slumber, with a tenacity that trembled upon the earth a certain uncharmed innocence: a stunning season, all sour.

She stood in her weight, her fallen arms at her sides: from the shoulder, she was ill-proportioned, as if she had come out headfirst and been pulled out of the womb in a hurried, fixated rush.

Her hair, plaited and clean, devoured the gleam and steadiness of her face. It was thick and heavy, crawled down the edge of her collarbone: a powerful, rigid announcement.

She closed her eyes and waited for Curtis to come this morning. He was of the earth now, and at any minute he'd come walking through the terror of the woods and hold her gleaming.

This was where she stood and waited: near the bed of this square and empty room.

A whisper crept into her eardrum: the white men had called Curtis from the house. But before the happening, he had turned and whispered, as he had each morning: "Now I know why the Garden of Eden was so beautiful. There was a woman in the middle of it."

She felt him, Curtis, standing behind her nude and poised body. He had come from the woods, past the maple tree, to tell it to her again and again for as long as she lived in this house and longed to hear it.

She burst into a laughter that belonged to no enemy. It shook her belly and she wanted so badly for him to touch her with his living and full hand that was no longer dead and swollen from the pulley. She formed it in her mind, the living hand, and imagined it enveloping her from the bone: it was as remarkable as she had pictured it.

It was no dream.

Sonny had seen the white boy run through the space of the woods. He was coming of age, the symptoms of history trailing behind him.

She was in blue, a wailing shape to the fabric that held no courtesy.

Her heart, as calm as it had been in the early morning, pounded with vigor: it was unexpected, the traveling boy.

She ran to the edge of the plotted earth, ran with her bare and protruding feet to the opening in the woods: the boy had escaped her, his yellow hair divided by the bark of a thousand trees.

She had not run far from the house before the dust caught her.

Trapped there, as the round eye of a hog: she panted into the wailing and dotted blue of her dress. She had not figured in her mind how immobile she was at that moment.

Sonny had not removed herself from the dust: she lay trembling and crooked in the blue wailing fabric, a coldness of the shoulder—she turned, her face and clavicle apart of the same splendor.

She breathed outward and into the bed of her moaning.

The boy she had seen was coming of age in Bullock, Mississippi: he would soon have to call a man from his house and drag him, drag him until he loses an eye, until a caterpillar crawls out.

She sat up from the ground.

The boy was gone now.

She took up the blue, could only think: They will grind him into powder.

The voice of Earl Thomas rang through the loudspeakers of Bullock. This was when Sonny remembered that it was Sunday and had not calculated the missing element of her journey. No time with God, not since Curtis.

The night before the dragging, the Thomases had come up the road a piece. Emma New had brought pie: it singed throughout her careful and meditative footing an honest and decent odor.

The men were out on the porch: they had whispered, one to another, before Curtis Willow turned away, pointed to a pattern on the ground, as if to comment invisibly: That there's the free.

Curtis Willow could lie down in the river, take upon himself the blood he carried, the bones that were his and belonged to no other man in the world.

He wanted to leave this town, take Sonny and her things—the things they owned—on the train to Memphis, leave this town and the Hurry Bullocks: but he had seen a man his size and build at the train station beg for work in exchange for a ticket, how the conductor had cursed him, struck him about the face, until at last the Negro sifted through the emaciated darkness where his hand had begun to quiver.

Again Curtis Willow turned and pointed to the pattern on the ground and then to Earl Thomas and asked with transparency: Where's your free?

The question rotated in Earl Thomas's head.

Not now, Curtis, he thought. Not now.

He, too, wanted to take Emma New and her things, take her up, and this town, the Bullocks, they would burn. The weighted question hung upon him: what he knew of God, of the flesh, shook him terribly.

Curtis Willow, his hand on the surface of the wind, broke the sphere of the pattern, crushed and visible on the ground, and faced the window of the house, the moon and Earl Thomas: I'm going home, he whispered.

Sonny and Emma New were standing near the curtain when he said it.

At this moment, Sonny knew.

Tomorrow he would go down to the river.

* * *

It was midnight when the Thomases left for home. Shortly thereafter, Sonny lit a lantern next to the bed and stretched out her hand to Curtis: Hurry Bullock.

For this was how she learned the power of her vocabulary.

Curtis sat up from the bed and grabbed her finger. He referred to bones when he taught her the straight letters. When he taught her the curved ones, it was buffalo.

Hurry: two horizontal columns, invisibly aligned, had been drawn in the palm of Sonny Willow's hand with his fingertip, a line at the center. An upward turn, the two R's, the final letter of the first name, Y, a woman on the edge of a mountain.

A whisper erupted throughout the lighted room. The emergence of oxygen from Sonny's womb hung in the transparency of the globe, a moan. In her exhalation, she pushed the word out from her ribs.

And so it was done.

The final line, *Bullock.*

Heavy, ain't it? whispered Curtis.

She drew her hand inward, to her bosom: she could yet feel the shape of the *Hurry* and *Bullock* with completion, as if she had been burned by the spine of the lantern, as if the thing that had been drawn upon her hand was at once gasping from its invisible and glowing lung. Her hand up to the lantern, she closed it, her fist centered above the rising flame, the mountain cloud that she had reached up there where God, too, heard it.

chapter
six

Lenora Bullock had taken to her chair out on the porch: she added no more a face to the setting than the little pink carnation that lay faded and beaten at her side. This was what she used to stir the heat around her, when she was too slow and lazy about going inside the house to retrieve the paper fan.

No later than twelve'o'clock was she here, sitting, waiting for the mail to come from the post office: she was a she bastard. If there was ever a record that she was the wanted child of any couple, it had yet to come.

No news from Jackson. She had written letters over the years, addressed to the same person, a woman with a tiny Q in her name.

My name is Lenora T. J. Bullock, she wrote. *I am the daughter of two people. One man. One woman. The woman I no longer care for.*) *I'm trying to find my daddy, before your tea gets cold. Dignified, L.B.*

A profound weeping of her structure—no pink carnation, a pansy—tore through the definition of her weighted face. From petal to seed, the Homo sapien, the fixed and angular strategy of her bones) failed to resist the crutch of her burdened, ill-fated history.

Her eye. Her tiny, irregular mouth. Her bones. All of them had come from someplace that peered through a sparse and withered gene within her: a momentary vein, displaced and rude, had risen in the crux of her arm.

As now, she was brave and patted it with her index finger, so the voice of its temperature would die in her eardrum.

A birthmark, the shape of Belgium, sat on the left side of her cheek: it had come from her mother. She was sure of it.

When Hurry Bullock had taken her in, her pores were dirty, her face smeared with the grit of waiting: she was incredulous, the odorous dependence of a maternal stain.

For all the she bastards bore the tattoo of their mothers: they had been pushed from the vagina, out into the world, their lungs pulsating from the blow. The blood spatter, the inability of their faces to resist the stain, drew upon them the territory of their ill-belonging, the aboriginal separation of maternalism.

Lenora Bullock's face was clean when he said it, the indissoluble birthmark peering out: It's your birthmark come from her, L.T., said Hurry. A trick.

Now Lenora Bullock had found her sitting place behind the wheel of the sewing machine. Adam would be here soon. She was the Klan seamstress. It was Lenora who bought the white fabric in town and Lenora who fitted the boys for the ceremony of thirteen.

Had she any news—a letter, perhaps—from the woman with a Q in her name, she wondered if she ever would have met Hurry Bullock—a train depot, she had not eaten all day, weak from the ride when he found her—or found a place in the world to commit herself to.

They were both wavering with revelation: Hurry, born into a confusing, forced sort of privilege, and herself, unable to measure the genealogy that seemed to paralyze the thread of her feeble hair: it had begun to turn into a pale gloom.

Lenora turned from her sitting and looked out at the pink carnation—the first flower she had ever held—the first anything given her that was permanent.

For she had burned the birth certificate: she smothered her) birthmark.

If only in her mind.

Adam emerged from the woods, Midnight behind him.

Lenora stood fully from her sitting chair and walked out to the edge of the porch to bring him in. He followed her back inside the house, where the warm scent of the sewing machine rose throughout the devastating heat and collapsed.

You're right early, she said, pouring him a glass of lemonade.

Although she had addressed Adam, it had come to her, the name of the office where she sent the letters: Vital Life.)

He could not help but notice her awkward position, as if she preferred the gaze upon her to come from behind—the birthmark on the left side of her cheek had begun to pound in the heat.

She placed the lemonade in front of him and turned toward the narrow border of the kitchen door, signaling for him to stand against it.

A silence fell between them: Adam wondered if she had swallowed a needle.

But rarely did he talk to Lenora Bullock: the whole town knew where her mind was.

She parted the horizontal line in her lips for a moment: as she measured Adam's growing bones, excitement rose inside her; a peculiar fascination with her own measuring pushed the wind from her gut.

The mark of Adam's growth had been made on the border with a fine no. 2 pencil she had brought home from the post office.

She reached inside a wooden toolbox that lay on the kitchen table: the reflex of irritation showed on her face. She had discovered a hole where a darner needle had slipped through.

It was this darner needle, minute and familiar, that she had used to stitch the fabric of the boy who had called Curtis from his nest. At this moment—and perhaps never again—it entered her mind: the force of the catastrophe, how she had gone to town the evening the corpse arrived at Hurry's lab, the stench of his mutilated and porous body, the eye from the socket, the head all bloated and dirty.

It had begun here at the Bullock house.

A darner needle.

She stalled for a moment, her head spinning with the loss and impact of the instrument, how now she must find it, so the events, the horrific picture of a new dragging, a new boy to measure, must come to rest in her path.

Adam reached out to touch her, as if he would tuck whatever it was that upset her back into its place. He had begun to wonder what was the matter.

Adam, she whispered. Sunday . . . Sunday'll fit me.

She began to say, Not now, son. Some other time. It's memory I can't forget.

But he had felt the words in her energy and ran through the door of the lopsided house, past the flaw of the pink carnation, where Midnight awaited him.

Lenora Bullock stood near the window, looking out, her hand up to the birthmark bearing the resemblance of a singular, disjointed gene.

chapter

seven

Earl Thomas was in the center of the forest.

He had come to this place out of paranoia, a misplacement of thought and mind: he had been night-sleeping, his twitching eye moving rapidly beneath the lid, where he had fallen into a slumber that was too momentary to hold. And, by morning, had journeyed away from Emma New and the maple tree—the fat and ugly bird that hummed a bit, replacing the order of his dream.

The galloping horses, men had woken him.

He stood, the killing tree above him, fractured in a terrible gaze: the blood of Curtis was of dust and bone now. The bitter, unbearable happening shook with the blue note of a mourning lyric.

Right about here, he figured, was where they popped his eye out, the skull weak and tired from the pulley: Curtis had been bound at the feet, the pressure of his spine drawn downward where the neck—the weight of his head—grew into a profound mass of responsibility.

Earl Thomas stuck his thumb in the belly of the earth. He measured the symptoms of drought and dirt. His finger, up from the earth, followed a white line in the sky: abandoned by a buzzing machine.

Earl Thomas was made of clay and he knew it. He brought his hands up to his face. The singed dirt of his fingertip left a powdered stain on his cheek.

He stationed his foot on the root of the tree, the other on its round belly, and grabbed hold of a limb that propelled him as he climbed, climbed to the second limb and the one thereafter: he looked down to where his thumb had gone into the earth's center.

Why had he come here this morning? Perhaps, in some utter defiance, he wanted to prepare himself for a killing in this town. He was the next bone, the next body, the energy of horses and men binding him at the foot, his head too heavy to ban the pulley from the raging muscle of his torso.

He had pictured it, Curtis, a man his size and weight, a man his age and stature, succumbing to the blue note: Earl Thomas had presided over funerals, the black widow humming to the mourning and waged lyric, stricken by a stone to the head, heart.

He was up high now. The limb bore the signature of his position: he had begun to breathe from there, one hand on his thigh. Earth and sky had collided.

If Curtis had come from this part to hold Sonny in the morning time, he had not at all heard the panting of the ghost. The scent overtook him: the odor of the corpse.

The bloody, bloody stench of what it was to live and breathe as he was. Nigger blood was what they called it. Nigger blood hooked to the pulley and hurried through the world, as if the world must forget, simply, that men like him had ever at all breathed in this place.

He thought it in his mind: Emma New, the black widow, sobbing on the pew of Sweet Home Baptist Church, the distinct pattern of her breathing forcing the veil into a bland curtain. It was the mouth that quivered.

Not only this but the ballad was what he heard: the weaving announcement of the closed casket where the scent of the iron pulley could not take to oxygen. The released foot, in full detachment from the killing, held in his memory.

He did not see it, had not gone far enough into the ground below him. The darner needle had slipped out from the hem of Lenora Bullock's skirt. This was where she had lost it—she had gone to Hurry, had been sowing the folds of the white, when she pinned it to the fabric of her skirt. It had simply come undone.

A rushing event was upon him. A running four-footed animal coming toward him. It rumbled throughout the forest with a trampling that braced him there on the branch. He was too high to come down now.

He awaited the animal as he wondered just how dangerous it was for him to climb so high in the tree this morning.

He closed his eyes, his heart pounding in what he now realized was nigger blood, if it was a white man who accompanied the haunting sound.

Just then the animal came to a stop in the woods.

It was Midnight, dark and silent, who found him in his position.

But now the pounding of Earl Thomas's heart had caused him to lose his balance on the branch. He came crashing back to where his thumb had gone into the earth. The rib, the bone, cracked.

Midnight stood at a distance.

He stirred a moment and leaned toward Earl Thomas, his hind legs holding the blunt of his curiosity, and licked his face. For he had seen Earl Thomas and Emma New: he had followed the scent of the apple pie.

He and Earl Thomas were alone in the woods. Earl Thomas moaned, the pain of the rib throbbing in his gut. He brought his hand up to Midnight, and Midnight licked it.

Earl Thomas did not know it, but this gesture, his hand up to the animal's wet breathing, stirred Midnight's nostalgia: the scent of Emma New's apple pie, fresh from the morning, lay in the palm of Earl Thomas's hand.

Earl Thomas moaned again as Midnight struck out into a sharp and more passionate run through the forest. The animal panted with hurry throughout the wooded forest until he came to the opening where Emma New stood on the steps of the Thomas house, folding a sheet.

Midnight panted.

Emma New abandoned the sheet of her folding. What is it, boy? she asked.

Midnight barked wildly, turned toward the forest, then back to Emma New. He started for the woods again and returned to face Emma New, his face a cloud of danger.

What is it? she repeated.

Midnight returned to the opening, his tail wagging ferociously out of context.

Emma New ran inside the house and returned with a square-shaped medicine box: she simply believed him.

Midnight broke through the hot and torrid heat of Mississippi, Emma New behind him. Show me to 'm, she yelled.

She ran, with full strength, to the center of the earth: Midnight had begun to breathe in his trepidation, until he led her to Earl Thomas's broken rib.

She yelled throughout the silent forest, Earl!

Earl Thomas lay on his spine, his finger drawn to his side, as if to show her the matter of his hurt without speech.

Emma New knelt beside him, no thought of her tiredness, and lifted the fabric of his shirt. She felt it, the broken rib: it moved in his belly.

Emma New, said Earl Thomas. Emma New, they're gonna . . .

Hush, now, she whispered.

She pulled his arms out of the shirt and reached in the wooden box for the bundled gauze: she dismantled it. As it lay flat on the bed of her arm, she beckoned for Earl Thomas to try, as much as he had life in him, to straighten his back.

He grunted, slowly lifting the spine, as she drew the gauze around him, tightening the rib, with hope, back into its position: it would heal. The marrow was a long stitch. It would set the rib, reshape itself into the original placement of Earl Thomas's anatomy.

She was sure of it.

She helped him from the ground, his arm about her neck: Help me, she beckoned. Give me you.

Earl Thomas stepped out with his foot. She looked out to where Midnight's lungs had caught a steady wind: he stood for a moment, his eyes no longer filled with hurry, and walked for home.

She wished she had a bone to give him, and although it was no place for it, she looked down into the box she had carried with her free hand. There was nothing, nothing to give him.

Mercy, she whispered. Mercy.

chapter
eight

We are white men, born unto the earth
And land, which is ours and belongs to us, as
Free and <u>automatic</u> white men.
All niggers must be obedient.
They are not a part of the human thread,
But are animals and must be dragged from
Their properties and stricken from the
Blood of the nation.
The same thing goes for hypocrites.

Hoover Pickens's hair was wet.

The heat had drowned it.

There, above the words of the Klan's declaration, was a loose board on the third tier of the barn. It had fallen out of position: he measured it with his eye and stepped down from the ladder.

He walked toward the door that caged the tools and felt a roaring patch of hurt in his ribs: he lifted his shirt and found his breathing. The left lung had begun to throb.

Both he and Earl Thomas, at this moment, were in vivid synchronicity. But Hoover Pickens was unaware of this: a disjointed moan erupted from his parted lips.

He was obtuse: the heaving lung pushed his belly out a bit, as if, in some sort of sickening stimulation, he had become incredible.

Hoover, yelled D.D., time for supper.

She was on the steps of the house. An invisible clone of heat rose around her.

Hoover? she whispered, her round head on the column of the breakfast porch.

No sign of him.

Midnight lay behind her, awaiting Adam. The energy of his silence, what he had seen in the woods—the solid stone of rescue—created a murmur within his heart.

He was no longer familiar with the scent of D. D. Pickens. She had not comforted him since taking him in her arms to save Adam. She was ungrateful, dead.

D. D. Pickens, for the first time, felt the bitter gaze of this animal: a rotten and ill-fated disregard for the oxygen that allowed them, in unison, to breathe this air and temperature as hot and merciful as it was.

She went to touch him, her quiet hand above him: he snarled at her, as if to say in the language of creature and earth, It's come too late in the world.

Adam stood at the bottom of the stairs. He had seen the happening and walked toward the screen door where D. D. Pickens stood in full dress. He thought it in his mind, but it had not come out of him, the question: What have you done?

D. D. Pickens brought her hand to her hip and, in some awareness of detail, moved away from Midnight.

The hair of Midnight's spine was in disarray, straight up it stood, until D. D. Pickens was forever gone this evening. She closed the door of her bedroom.

When Midnight heard it, he returned to his original position, his warm belly on the bed of the breakfast porch: Adam had disappeared into the mouth of the barn.

Adam had only vaguely heard of what the other boy had done to Curtis: he was in the high window of the house when Salem and Hurry Bullock described the swollen torso, the bloated head.

It was no wonder that when Adam's father sent him to Hurry Bullock's lab the morning after the dragging, he vomited at the sight of the corpse: Curtis's body lay on a wooden gurney. The head had a hole it, and Hurry Bullock had stuck a pipe into it that had begun to whistle. It went straight from the back of the head through the hole in his eye. A whistling, pitiful sound that Adam could not hold in his stomach.

At once, the food he had eaten before coming was strewn from his esophagus and onto the cold, cold floor.

He recalled that evening: his father had sent him for the package of things. It was customary for the Klan of Bullock, Mississippi, to save the contents of a nigger's pockets.

His father wanted him to see it: the nigger blood and bone, the duty that awaited him. The power. The masterful work of the free and automatic white men.

Adam had run from Hurry Bullock's lab, the contents trembling in his little hand, only to find his father standing on the breakfast porch: an overt grin leaned into his face.

Adam dropped the package in front of him and ran up the stairs of the house, up to his room where the stench of his stomach had begun to levitate above the space he had collapsed into.

Now Adam stood in the barn's opening.

It was Sunday. Lenora Bullock had fitted him early this morning: free from memory and the darner needle, she had returned to the unremorseful place in her heart. And it was, indeed, Lenora Bullock who could not confine the whisper. She had been waiting on her letter from the Vital Life Office when she said it.

The line had been forwarded from her lips: You've got a killin' to do.

The news plagued Adam: he watched as his father rose from his hammering on the third tier and asked what brought him here.

As it was with Adam, he spoke: Miss Lenora says I gotta killin' to do.

Salem Bullock was out running the horses.

Hoover Pickens and Adam, alone, were in the stable.

She's good 'n' human, ain't she? Hoover Pickens sent the hurling phlegm of a cough into the barn dust.

Adam saw it, blood: How long're you gonna live, Pa?

Long enough to do some mercy, said Hoover Pickens.

Who's gotta ask for it?

Hoover Pickens had replaced the wooden board of the third tier and was now near the tier's edge: A nigger's gotta ask for it. That's who.

How come he can't just go straight to the Lord 'n' get it? asked Adam.

The question struck Hoover Pickens in the lung from which he had coughed: the leaking organ forced a gap in his behavior.

Midnight howled from the breakfast porch.

Son, urged Hoover Pickens. A nigger . . . A nigger's gotta . . .

Before this line could consume both boy and man, Adam looked down at the phlegm that had come from his father's lungs and interrupted: Pa, he said. There's blood in it.

Hoover Pickens turned away from the tier's edge: Yes, son, he said. Blood.

The pulsating line struck the invisible, perplexed earth between them.

Adam's head had begun to hurt, the world.

Hoover Pickens stepped down from the ladder to the ground floor of the barn where Salem Bullock was returning: he reached out to Adam.

But Adam had walked back toward the house: he had discovered the debilitating ode of obedience, of constitution, entrapment.

chapter

nine

The sky woke with rain.

Emma New was nebulous and distorted in her thinking this morning. At once she was indistinguishable from the earth. A feathered bird.

Mended by rib and gut, she was in the center of the Thomas house: she stood in her position, her vertebrae moving forward.

Earl Thomas was asleep.

Emma New stood above him. His breathing was in this room. If ever he had lived in his freedom, it was at this moment.

It was protection she could not give him.

So alive he was at this moment that she closed her eyes and hollered as loud and disquietly, in her mind, as to give no attention to herself, but to sound.

Come out yonder, they'd say. Come out yonder.

For when Curtis Willow looked at the ground, pointed, she thought of the news, nearly thirteen years ago: a son had been born unto Hoover Pickens and he would rise up and drag the nigger who'd come up to the Pauer Plant; the boy who'd do the dragging had to be his and come from him, so the nigger'd know—after all these years—what a frivolous thing he'd done.

Soon Earl Thomas would point here or there, and it would be his ground and earth. And he would turn, face her: Emma New, he'd say, I'm going home.

How she'd begged him to leave this town, take her up to Memphis—something about God, he moaned—God and duty. The arrangement of the line, the narrow and intimate words burned in her throat. And although it was temporary, God, God burned, too.

She recalled asking him all those years ago: What do you think they'll do? as she stared at the letter. Read it, see how short they hope is, 'n' kill us all? Or see how dead they is 'n' live?

Her questioning was not isolated: in her rhetoric, she spoke not only to Earl Thomas but to the government. Those who had sent the letter were somewhere, slumbering, and in their slumber, she stood invisibly at their feet, said: He's my blood, bone. If they dead, let Him tell it.

She remembered, too, Earl's looking down at the letter, his panting, his confusion.

The pattern on the ground was his.

Now Emma New paused in the room, Earl yet sleeping.

Perhaps if she'd asked Sonny how they'd done Curtis, how they'd called Curtis from the house, she'd know by now how to handle . . . death. But she would never ask Sonny, she'd only bake her a pie in the oven or pull a dress over her bones to protect herself from it: *lung wind* was what she called it.

The age and hope of a nigger were less than redeeming, especially now, when it seemed Earl Thomas was more alive than they imagined him.

A broken rib. A fall from a tree. If this was all it was, she could live in his safety. She had tools for such things: a broken rib, a fall from a tree.

A dragging. Curtis. She had not asked Sonny, but she well knew how it had happened. Curtis had been in the woods, an undistilled moment between white woman and nigger: Lenora Bullock had run to her house, her dress all torn up . . . That nigger. Curtis Willow had done it.

Even a whistle. A whistle had come from the nigger's lips and he left me there, half-naked and hungry. You oughta take 'm to the Mississippi, drown him, said Lenora Bullock.

Sonny had run through the woods, come for Emma New, her face ripped of lung wind: she had hollered there on the steps of the Thomas house only a short while before her limbs came to a pause.

Curtis was dead.

A wheelbarrow. Curtis's bloated head. The body stiff and naked where even his penis had begun to swell.

They had wheeled him through town, daylight, and into Hurry Bullock's office: they threw him together, chiseled him into grit. Sonny, she got the bones.

Emma New was without privacy: she had begun to shiver.

The thought of it: a wheelbarrow.

Only her head kept still: she had drawn her mouth to a close.

She turned, with hurry, away from Earl Thomas's slumber: his odorous body, blood on the trees.

The rain had stopped, and she alone was alive in the house. She had no power.

A rotten tree, a root, had been carved into her belly. Earl Thomas, Curtis, hung from it. The stench of rigor mortis. She was no good without it. Memory.

Her nose began to bleed.

The blood fell onto her gown, the floor.

Earl Thomas had begun to stir. She ran out of the room and into the face of a horizontal and dirty mirror that hung over a vanity table near the kitchen sink: of all the places to put it. She thought herself religious. And there, streaming and bulbous in her nostril, was the incredible scent of blood.

A tiny napkin lay beside her. She brought it up to her face: the blood came out in her breathing. All stained now.

The sound of the horses took her out of place and position: the Bullocks, Hoover Pickens, had come to a halt near the maple tree.

Perhaps it was her brave and utter tiredness that caused her to bring her finger up to her face, over the edge of her lips, as if to say: Be quiet. My husband is sleeping.

The bare weight of the white men's bodies moaned until earth and rain were mute.

Hurry Bullock brought his horse up to the window. Emma New turned for a moment; Earl Thomas had not woken from his slumber. And with her finger yet pressed on her lips, she met both man and horse there.

Hurry Bullock, his depressing and round figure, was so confined in her head that she dropped the napkin at her feet. She looked down upon it.

And with her head bowed, he spat in her face.

The others, Hoover Pickens and Salem Bullock, raised their horses. *Nigger* was what they said. *Nigger*. And took to their horses, the laughter of Hurry Bullock leading them back to the cave.

Emma New? said Earl Thomas.

Why had he only now waked? She had gone through all the symptoms of misery there while he was sleeping. A nosebleed. The spit of Hurry Bullock that had turned her face into a drum.

Emma New?

Even in his slumber, under the restraint of the elixir she had given him, he should have woken with the horses, the sound of

white men. He should have come to, she thought, out of protection, when I took such a blow to keep him safe.

She had not turned from the window: she took it. The spit. The
white men and their horses. She looked down at her feet again.
The napkin lay like the rustling tune of a wheelbarrow.

Sleep, she uttered. A chain pulled out o' the Mississippi.

Earl Thomas lay in bed, wondering if pus was in his rib, and
knew that he could not ask her to turn when the frequency of her
breathing, the calm arrow of a woman's lung wind, had caused her
to take it.

chapter
ten

Emma New rose from the porcelain bathtub, naked and wet.

She would be sick by morning: her housecoat had not even been removed.

The weaving cloud of a lantern led her away from the Thomas house.

She journeyed, past limb and tree, to Sonny's. The moon was pregnant: a carelessness had begun to jut out from its glowing, as if it had been drawn there, tied to a string, a kite.

Perhaps it had reached into her gown—where the breast was— and wondered how women like her, the Emma News of the forest, could at all succumb to misery when the presence of common sense should have moved them to another town.

But of course Emma New, throughout her begging Earl Thomas to leave this place, had seen the nerve of his temple hold in his face when he moaned: God sent me to take it.

She paused in her walk. The body of Emma New purred from the bone: the pure nature of the buzzing leaned her forward like a porcelain cup.

She balanced the leaning buzz in her round head. With her hand up to her breast, she felt a grand, haunting memory. The buzz had landed.

The lantern began to wheeze, low kerosene.

The kerosene descended into a whisper in her hand.

She measured the circumference of the whisper to that of her breast and stretched out her hand, as if air and night would guide her to Sonny's house. She thought a door had opened, a woman— no one else but Sonny at this hour—must've walked out of it.

She yelled: Sonny?

One step into this rich and pitiful darkness she had found herself in. One giant step and she would've known how silly she had been to call out for a ghost.

For no one had opened a door.

Not Sonny. Not the house she had left behind. And not the Pickens's house.

Everyone was dreaming of rain.

She alone was left: the wooded forest had gone to sleep.

She was out here, at this distant hour, with her hands stretched out like an outdated and vigorous purpose that lies exposed to earth and the elements and comes out sour.

The crickets had begun to chirp and rotate: their rambling fits of chatter sat still in her face and she shook it, she shook her face, and stepped forward.

She imagined the sound of the dragging, Curtis calling out to Sonny and the white men and their horses . . . the pulley was what she imagined, really, how drawn it was to the hind leg . . . her depiction stained her reasoning, turned it into something dirty.

Sonny? she yelled.

She could've collapsed in her calling until Sonny heard it in her sleep—Sonny?—and stepped out from her porch.

Emma New had begun to run now, run, run past tree and limb to the opening in the woods.

Sonny?

Here, Emma New, said Sonny. Here.

Sonny had not reached for her gown. She was yet naked, as she had been in her slumber: her breasts like the belly of a hummingbird, narrow and downward in motion.

Curtis had been called from the house around this hour, midnight: she had worn a battered, strict gown with a dirty gardenia on it. And now, when she slept, she slept naked, so no one—not even the white men—could cause her to suffer.

Emma New sat on the edge of Sonny's bed, breathing wildly.

Sonny lay beside her from behind, the punctured gap of her cellulite exposed.

Emma New, she whispered. Why you not sleep with the rest o' the world?

Emma New, embarrassed in her insomnia, had abandoned the lantern at the steps and was now apart of a witty daze that strung its rude district around her battered breathing.

Sonny, she panted, I dream.

What you dream of, Emma New? asked Sonny.

It moans, whispered Emma New. I can't shake it. I can't shake it, Sonny.

Sonny turned her head to the window: Curtis would come in the morning and stand behind her and whisper something sweet like *There was a woman in it* and all this weak woman-talk would slide down her shoulder and burn.

Did he holler? asked Emma New.

No.

Did he beg for mercy? asked Emma New.

From God.

What you do when you heard it?

Sonny turned to her pillow as if she wanted to taste her disturbed sleep. I . . . she added . . . I don't remember quite. I think I put my hands together and grinned. God had done touched 'm.

Emma New had caught her lung wind and paused in her sudden and trampled questioning.

Sonny, said Emma New, he broke a rib.

The best part, replied Sonny.

But she wanted to say: A rib is what he broke? A rib done give 'm by God, made to heal and be? The only bone they can't take. Complimentary.

Sorrow had gone so far down, down there where things break and get easy: Sonny remembered the night she woke up—the matters of her face dispersed—the night she realized Curtis was not in the house: a hanging was what they would do.

He had been out in moon-air, up in the forest tree, when he asked the moon for it, God who lived in the moon, to get him and Sonny to Memphis: he knew men there who worked on the railroad. He could find work, buy Sonny a new gown.

But the moon was awake only in his eye, and it was the moon who had not at all heard him.

A bird come this mornin', said Sonny. You couldn't tell it from the sky who brought it. All the time free.

She thought of Curtis.

Nothing left, she whispered. Bones.

Emma New, her shoulder heavy and wet, had begun to weep.

Love him like he dead, said Sonny.

Sonny stood away from the bed, Emma New trembling.

The space around them became a thing of spirit to Sonny, as she had already done her crying. She had already done her weak woman-talk. She had done it near the window where God and Curtis heard it.

She reached out to Emma New: Come, she whispered.

Emma New stood to her feet: she and Sonny walked over to the open window.

The stars had begun to emerge, a planet within them, an entire universe, when Sonny took Emma New's index finger and pointed to the galaxy of milk surrounding the slumber of men and horses and rib: Love him like he dead.

Emma New traveled through the woods again, the kerosene from Sonny's lantern guiding her without hurry back to the house of her restlessness where Earl Thomas awaited her, his rib glowing.

chapter
eleven

A dead nigger had lain frozen in Hurry Bullock's morgue: a tiny hole in the throat. The yellow eye of morbidity. The skull was crushed: a caterpillar crawled out of his head.

Hoover Pickens and Salem Bullock surrounded the corpse.

Hurry Bullock had given them a substance, greaselike, that lay beneath their nostrils to guard them from the rotting head, the bare positioning of the brain: the matter was exposed now, a blow to the cranium.

The room was morbid, the unbearable arrangement of chemicals: everything began with a consonant: J for jungle. JB for jungle blood. JP for jungle piss.

The shelves were disproportionate to Hurry Bullock's height. He reached up high on the shelf for the tools that he'd used to privately puncture an already dead lung, a penis. The bones of the throat.

In the morning time, only Hurry Bullock and the corpse occupied the room—in some grand and striking matrimony—as if he could not help that it was so close.

There lived within him an accuracy for violent and devastating behavior: he knew where to let the JP out, how to take what piss was left of the corpse and drain it from the penis. The jungle blood ran down the sewerage, through towns like Bullock and Pyke County, Mississippi: the stench, he wanted it to linger in the permanent body of wind and earth, so the niggers, so God could take it down, down through the nostril and swallow his power.

Where'd they catch 'm? asked Hoover Pickens.

In the river, said Hurry Bullock.

He drowned, yelled Salem Bullock, whose laughter rose through the morbid room with a determination that so struck the irredeemable structure of his body that it caused his foot to lean forward.

They all held their bellies, the Bullocks and Hoover Pickens, laughing this way with their disastrous and haunting gills, as the corpse lay before them: the swollen gene of some mother's donation to the world had become a blunt and horrible ruse.

There lived an entire fascination for the tongs that Hurry Bullock plunged into the lung of the corpse—not dead enough—that the screams and laughter and niggers and *He drowned* caused the oxygen of the room to confine itself to the corpse, as if the corpse itself had begun to breathe.

How they laughed and turned their faces to the dead, laughed in circulation: none of them thought of it—the pins could come loose from the dead man's hips—he could rise in his deadness, his upper body erect and plausible.

A drowning. A drowning had done it. He had gone down in the river and had his lung punctured, his earlobe dismantled, leg broken, and the face, no one could tell his age, and of course, the eye, a drowning had done that, too.

Turn 'm over, said Salem Bullock.

Hoover Pickens said, Yeah, Hurry, turn 'm over. We wanna see it.

They longed to witness the vertebrae: a man was dragged through the woods, the ground ripped through his shirt, bare skin on earth, and came down on the spine like a welding tool.

Hurry Bullock, white-gloved, caught the stiffness of the corpse and moved the body onto its stomach. There it was, the chiseled and boned vertebrae of the jungle bone.

That was what they called it.

In a collective degree of expansion, their shoulder blades began to rotate.

Jungle blood, whispered Hurry Bullock.

Why had the corpse terrified them so? They could not imagine entrapment, waking up in the morning with a nigger's bones. The symptoms of Darwinism, apes and Homo sapiens, hung above the constitution. Put there by their fathers and grandfathers and those before them like an unattainable guide to the redemptive peace of hate.

Hatred had lived so inevitably—an inward and satisfactory progress—within their systematic bodies that it swiveled like a heavy and sour plate struck down on the breakfast porch.

Within measure, the room embodied them and the rustic scent of the corpse began to rise through the greaselike air beneath their nostrils and Hoover Pickens breathed it all in, the stench of the corpse, and leaned over from the gut and vomited.

It had risen up from his acidic stomach, and as it streamed out of him, he hoped no one had seen it, the food that had rotted in his stomach from the heat.

Salem Bullock stood behind him and patted him on the shoulder.

Hoover Pickens lifted his hand to the sour oxygen of his mouth and turned away from the corpse and went out of the room where he could breathe. He walked out of the morgue and could hear them, the Bullocks, laughing and saying it again, over and over they said it: Weak.

They had seen it come out of him, the vomit, how fragile his stomach was. This alone concerned him.

The Bullocks joined him in the night air.

That's what happens when you mix jungle blood with the pure, said Salem Bullock. Wet.

Better you than Adam, said Hurry Bullock.

Hoover Pickens never told it. But Adam *had* done his vomiting: he had delivered the contents of Curtis Willow's pocket to him. He could smell the sour odor on Adam's breath, the contour of his stomach bellowing, his gut empty.

The boy who had called Curtis from his house hadn't at all vomited, at least there was no word of it. A boy was to hold it, all therein, and take it, take it like a man and member of the free and automatic men.

Hoover Pickens had not told Adam how he would have to call the next nigger from his house, drag him on the ground until the bloody corpse lay in the woods, the head trembling on the edge of a wheelbarrow in the morning time.

Hurry Bullock looked down at his foot. An object had begun to shine in the moon glow. He reached for it, dust-fingered. A dime.

He dropped it in his pocket and shook it until the vibration struck his thigh. Night, boys, he said, before disappearing back into the morgue.

Hoover Pickens did not respond.

He walked over to his horse and jumped on top of it.

Hurry Bullock stood near the window and watched as Hoover Pickens kicked his horse in the ribs, yelled out—Ya!—in the direction of the forest, a trail of vomit behind him.

chapter
twelve

A white dress, tied at the shoulders, covered Lenora Bullock's body with the delicate and wilted quality of a crooked vein. Her hand went up to her face, as if to signal to the sun's interrogation to leave her alone.

She had traveled away from the porch and now stood in the dust.

Hurry Bullock was out in his own barn this afternoon: he had not asked for her intrusion—she had come to his bedside each morning—a poke to the side.

Wake up, Hurry, she'd say. Time for breakfast.

He had thought of opportunity: at once his hand could rise, make contact with her eye, and send her spurring down the steps of the house.

No one would care. An orphan.

And her *Wake up, Hurrys*, her *Time for breakfasts*—her rude and barbaric vocabulary—would swivel in her elongated head, right behind the eye, and pin her down.

A dirty gardenia.

Lenora Bullock yet quivered from it: Before his trip to the barn, he had come out of the house, shaken his head at the dress, and pulled the strap loose until her right breast fell out.

That's what you get, he whispered. Bastard.

There were moments when he wished he'd left her at the train station: he should've known that she was an orphan. Her birthmark had a smudge of red on it where her hand was so out of focus that the lipstick traveled up the side of her jawbone. Perhaps it was because she looked so pitiful, an unprofessional clown, that he brought her home.

He would no sooner admit his loneliness when he found her than he would the ticking lung that lifted him out of bed this morning and made him cough.

She had only just now bridged herself together: the letter had not come from the Vital Life Office yet. She wished it'd hurry.

How brave she had been, the sun of this afternoon pelting down on her solidity, as it motioned in front of her dress-shadow: she had spent hours sewing it, her first daring creation, to draw some kind of attention.

She raised her arms: they were outstretched and balanced about her, as if she wanted to prove to the world her vulnerability. But there, in the dress-shadow, her fingers paused in movement.

Gravity.

She was already home, already the wife of Hurry Bullock who'd found her at the train station. Her carelessness was as bound to her spirit as the profound displacement of the darner needle.

She brought her arms to her hips and leaned downward. The expression of her face, she could put her finger up to her head, pretend that it had entered through the eardrum, and everyone would notice, everyone would pay attention. She'd be in the dust.

She'd be dead.

Soon Adam and Midnight would emerge from the wooded forest.

She had sent word to D. D. Pickens. Send Adam, she said. I've got an errand needs tending to.

Hurry Bullock stood in the barn's opening: Comp'ny? he asked.

Lenora Bullock, wife of Hurry Bullock and seamstress, fell into the debate of a momentary grin: Adam, she replied.

She stood in the unknown history of her bones: how ungrateful and cunning she was that she would remark upon his questioning with such arrogance when he could have easily done it this morning, slapped her face.

He wiped the sweat from his forehead and disappeared.

Adam and Midnight, each breathing heavily, arrived from the forest.

The sun had trapped the hour of Adam's breathing: he squatted before Lenora Bullock, the dress-shadow and heat combined around him, as if she had all of a sudden drawn him into the exposed breast, the red smear going up the side of her jawbone.

Mama says you've got something needs doing, he panted.

She turned away for a moment. She could offer him lemonade fresh from the cooler, but not at such a time, when something employable and fascinating had come out of this: it was opportunity, the scent of his breathing, that caused her to face him again.

An odor of derision whistled from his nostrils: she was inhaling the oxygen of a boy who belonged to two living people.

She took it all in.

Adam looked up at her from the dust. Miss Lenora? he asked.

She leaned in her words: I need a darner needle. Go to the fabric store 'n' tell the clerk that you come to get Lenora Bullock a darner needle. Tell her to pin it to your collar.

Yes, 'm.

Keep your hand up to your collar, so it'll keep, she said.

Yes, 'm.

Midnight had done his panting and rose with Adam through the forest again.

Lenora Bullock stood where they had left her, the dust of their sudden abandonment rising around her like the powdered wind of chiseled vertebrae.

Adam left Midnight behind—he had found a bone—and marched up the steps of the fabric store: it was adjacent to the post office and echoed the brittle, dilapidated posture of a weep-ing drunkard.

Good Adam. You're hope, Adam. Take 'm down, Adam. The men pounded his shoulder with their vocabulary as he passed through the wooden door of the fabric store: he could tell by their breathing that they had brought the bird down.

He walked up to the counter, rang the bell.

The clerk had been playing a piano in the rear of the fabric store. Her fingers parted in separation from the keys, the final edge of a tune pausing.

Now she appeared before Adam, her pink face stripped of ac-curacy; if she had known at all why she was alive, it would have lived in the activity of the muscle that rose throughout the pale ferocity of her standing place, turned her into salt.

Miss Lenora Bullock sent me for a needle, said Adam. Says to pin it to my collar.

What kind? asked the clerk.

A darner.

The clerk stood near a cashier's drawer; the horizontal counter separated her from this boy who seemed, in her opinion, to have made the whole place sour.

Of course she knew him, the son of D. D. and Hoover Pickens, the next boy to bloody up the woods with his calling: she'd have to witness it again, the wheelbarrow as it passed the window, the arm hanging out of it. A nigger's corpse.

84

She reached behind her. A wagon wheel of embroidered fabric, pansies, hung from a lead pipe attached to the ceiling. She had labeled each set of needles pinned to the material, until she saw it, the word she had herself written: DARNER.

A metallic thimble covered her thumb as she thought to herself, some sort of method she had acquired: Lenora Bullock. DARNER. Klan.

The meditation of her inward vocabulary halted, and she pulled a darner needle from a lavender pansy and gave it to Adam.

She did not say *Good boy, Adam, You're hope, Adam, Take 'm down, Adam,* but instead pinned the darner needle to his collar and laid her pink hand on the counter, as if to say: *I'm done with you.*

By this time, the mail clerk, in the adjacent window of the post office, walked up to the square-shaped glass and flipped over a sign that read: OUT TO LUNCH.

He was of shocking quality: a cancerous germ had eaten into the lower edge of his jawbone, and he kept his hand up to his face to hide his disfigurement.

Chewing tobacco.

He had, many times, wondered why he had stayed so long in public when he had to constantly bring his hand down to reach for the letters in their cubicles.

He felt it: they whispered about his vulnerability. A freak.

Adam had come out of the fabric store, Midnight beside him.

The post office clerk took him by the shoulder, a white government envelope in his hands. He saw the darner needle in Adam's collar.

Going out to the Bullocks, I figure, he said, his hand up to his face.

Yes, sir, said Adam.

He looked away from the post office clerk with the low self-esteem of a boy with his own solitary burden to keep.

This come for Lenora, said the post office clerk.

Adam took the envelope and watched the dizzying limp of the post office clerk: the thing that disfigured him had passed through his intestines and into the unstable predictability of his footsteps.

The post office clerk was of no use to the world: a horse trapped in barbed wire.

Adam had found his way through the center of the forest when Midnight paused.

Earl Thomas had fallen from this tree, his rib loose in his gut.

What's a matter, boy? asked Adam.

Midnight stepped away from him and turned.

What's a matter, boy? asked Adam. Weak?

Midnight howled, ran in a separate direction, and stopped, waiting for Adam to follow.

Adam's hand was on the darner needle now. It was yet pinned to his collar.

He faced Midnight, his head sideways: trust.

He followed Midnight through the forest, the sun peering above them.

Midnight halted.

There it was, the Thomas house, far away but visible from the opening: Emma New and Earl Thomas were on the porch of their house, her arm hitched around his full waist. His rib had begun to heal.

Adam's presence went unseen as he knelt down to the earth: he had seen the corpse lying stiff and naked in Hurry Bullock's morgue. The swollen head, the castrated penis, how it all sat in his head right now and shaped itself into being.

The corpse. Had it been the normal fitting, the normal calcu-lation of a man its height, it would have looked like Earl Thomas, before the swelling, before the eye had come loose.

It was no wonder the white envelope from the Vital Life Office slipped right out of his pocket and onto the ground.

Adam trembled: a red-haired boy, turned man, had followed him from town. He had been in the post office before the clerk left for lunch, had seen the letters on the envelope from the Vital Life Office.

A lady with a Q in her name had sent it.

The follower reached down beside Adam and took up the letter.

Hurry Bullock, he commented. He's the one. The ringleader. I can't even sleep these days.

Midnight had not barked upon the stranger's arrival: he knew him.

Five years ago now that it happened.

Curtis Willow. Dead.

Midnight, in the language of his other world, remembered how the red-haired boy's father had slapped him wildly: they made him hook Curtis to the pulley and drag him, drag him through the wooded forest, until the unbalanced terrain of the earth burned his vertebrae into grit.

Come with me, whispered the stranger, the envelope in his pocket.

Adam, a vast curiosity within him, walked quietly behind.

They returned to the center of the forest.

The stranger paused: Name's Gill, he said. Ever heard o' me?

Adam shook his head.

Gill towered above Adam with a confining strength, haunting in its exhibitory manner, that reeked of violent and disturbing synchronicity. His hands were large and powerful, as if memory had spun him into independence.

Cowards, he said. They haven't told you, have they?

No.

Gill had waited years for this meeting. He had found work on the railroad collecting the tickets of women like Lenora Bullock who landed in this town, grew into Klan wives and seamstresses. He hated them, their childlike save-me faces, how they stood before him with false arrogance—pretending someone was coming to get them, smudged and dirty.

His father had gotten his mother from the train station: he was a railroad baby, fresh and plucked from the sitting orphanage. He hated them, too: the mother for not stopping the whole thing, his father for pushing, pushing, pushing—all that they'd made him do.

He turned his back to Adam and took a letter opener from his pocket, breaking the seal of the envelope: after reading the contents, he broke with laughter.

Of course he knew, as did the whole town, that Lenora Bullock had waited her entire life for this moment: his foot leaped forward (as if to pound the news of her father into the ground.

He paused, facing Adam: Tell 'er you lost it.

The lie drove a nail into Adam's eardrum.

The clerk's got surgery, said Gill. Nobody to deliver the mail.

If Adam had stood at the counter a moment longer, he would have heard the announcement from the post office clerk: It's come back. I'm shutting down.

It was this clerk, the only fit person in Bullock to stack the items of delivery, who gave the keys to the woman at the fabric store: she had agreed to pass the word out.

The sign had been blurry, did not read OUT TO LUNCH, but OUT FOR A LONG TIME, before the post office clerk walked away from the womb of the town, his hand up to his lower mandible, and disappeared.

You never saw me, said Gill.

But he would return to the Pickens's house, where he had not been since Curtis, and reestablish himself with the free and automatic white men.

Lenora Bullock lifted the darner needle from Adam's collar and poured him a glass of lemonade, his genetic breathing more potent and credible with thirst.

chapter
thirteen

Nigger, come out yonder.
There's gonna be a killin' in this town.

Earl Thomas woke from the nightmare.

How it dizzied him: the rotting carcass of his slumber lay down below—muddy—the head turned agape, the lips immobile, as if the final moan of his discomfort shook the cage of his larynx into a startling, full-blown expression of mercy.

He was so heavy now: his shoulders, in contrast to the things in the room, echoed a terrible sort of symmetry. He sat up from the pillows and wondered for a moment how he had come to this place.

Emma New was a blur. She disappeared into the kitchen and returned with a pair of iron shears. Lay down, she whispered. Easy.

The sweat of his nightmare rose from the gauze of his ribs.

Emma New, he repeated. Emma New . . . they.

She lifted her finger to her lips.

If he could tell her that he had seen the carcass. The round and bloody head had begun to swell. The peculiar setting of the feet, the pulley had upset the rotation of the ankle.

The face, the face was what he could not see.

But of course he knew it was his.

Emma New, he pleaded. Let me tell it.

She stopped her shearing of the gauze: Tell it to God, Earl Thomas, she said. Nothing *I* can do. Flesh.

She held it inward, Sonny's adopted line: Love him like he dead.

A grin eased her, and she returned to the shearing of the gauze: Sister Harriet come by this morning, she whispered.

He turned away from Emma New, interrupted.

Emma New continued: Says it's a pity to leave Baptists waitin'.

He had not thought of the Baptists or his Sunday preaching. But it was God, God who entered his nightmares, whispered: I sent my only Son to take it. Now you, too, must.

The line flew above him like the tail of a kite loosed from the limb of a giant bird.

Was there ever such a thing in the world that he would be so set to the rhythm of agony within him that he seemed even more out of tune?

It was all too shocking to hold, both lines—*There's gonna be a killin' in this town* and *Now you, too, must*—that they repeated themselves, one with victory, one with such repulsion, that the language of the two things, the two constitutions, rolled him into a bare and complex position on the pillows.

There, said Emma New, pointing.

A hummingbird fluttered in the window. The belly obtuse, as if it had swallowed the milk of a breast that hung in its species like the distant subtlety and chimera of illusion.

Emma New had cut the gauze entirely and eased it out from under Earl Thomas's rib. Look what the Lord done, she said.

He caught his lung wind. It occurred to him how trapped

he had been, a mummy. He breathed heavily, his hand on his gut.

He had been let go of: the gauze had weighed him down in his sleep.

He could run now, faster and quicker than the white men. He could keep running until the horses tired, until the boy—his There's-gonna-be-a-killin'-in-this-town talk—would succumb to the sweat of his waking.

His lung wind had begun to slow down.

It again struck him: I sent my only Son to take it. Now you, too, must.

He lay there for a time—Emma New bound to the obtuse belly of the hummingbird, the gown pulled down to her waist, her breasts exposed—and reached beside him.

The rotting ink of the outdated letter was yet in his pocket. *To the Men of the Pauer Plant,* it read. *Courtesy of the Pastor.* It shook him as if he were a minute, undefined detail: a stroke of the wrist, a matter of swarming news, and send it out to the nigger in Bullock, Mississippi.

They're all the same.

Now he remembered how the news had fascinated him: Hoover Pickens and the Bullocks, the free and automatic white men who worked in the factory, all of them were . . . dust.

He looked over at Emma New, the fluttering hummingbird hidden behind her standing, her head aside with amazement.

The house held their quiet.

He could, at any moment, burst out into laughter, away from the house, the hummingbird in its thirst, and bid them dead: the white men, the needles metastasizing.

But it was not his laughter that broke the quiet: it was Emma New's.

In her sweet and utter standing, her voice broke. How it lingered for a time near the window, the hummingbird and its flutter gone now.

Emma New? whispered Earl Thomas.

But she did not answer him, as he did not wake from his slumber when Hurry Bullock spat in her face. She was separate from world and bait. A sudden relief had overcome her—without explanation and pity.

Surely he had heard the roaming horses at the window: he had seen Hurry Bullock spit in her face. That particular morning, he had done nothing and, in the falseness of his slumber, had asked himself inwardly: What have I done?

He hoped she would turn: the hummingbird had taken all of it, nothing left.

There stood in sky and earth a galaxy, an ornamental pattern of stars that surrounded themselves in Emma New's profound laughter: the elements of her attention began to remark upon her a kind of redemptory setting of the bones. She had begun to move, her face up to the lighted globe, the moon running down the tongue. Like milk.

Nothing would happen in this house that was not hers: the elements of earth and sky gathering about. Indeed, in her poise, she heard it.

Swallow, it urged. Take it all down.

Earl Thomas abandoned the rotting ink.

He wondered, if this was what it was to be unbound—annihilated and let go of—then he would rather have the weight of the gauze, the mere suffocation of the lung, take part in his living.

Emma New. What was happening to her? How had she come to this? The treatment of him, as though he were dead.

He commented: Emma New, come to bed.

And thus she turned, lifted the paralysis of her gown up to her breasts, and slid under the covers, the scent of milk and pansy adrift where Earl Thomas, in his Emma New abandonment, reached out and brought her in.

His rib no longer throbbing but idle.

chapter
fourteen

Sonny stood, like the dust of anthropology, in earth and heat.

She had come to a point of immobility outside her house, the sun in her mouth.

She had seen a boy from the window, running there in the woods.

Her mouth opened as if to conjoin the sighting with the conspiracy of earth and heat: the shape of Curtis grew into memory.

Within her fell a pouch of diction, tongue-language, that rose from her stomach and into dust and cloud. Her voice, trembling and drumlike, shook with vibration, hurry.

Nothing could stop this sound. Far-reaching it was, so that it ricocheted away from her bone and body, and over the Thomas house: Emma New heard it and paused in her work. Sonny. Sonny's remembrance of the dead.

The tune had crystallized in Sonny's throat.

Perhaps Curtis had found his way to her tongue-language. Perhaps it was the memory of Curtis that had found it: she felt him running, running through the forest, all fixed, and waited for the spirit to leap out behind her, hold her steady.

The calling hung in her eardrums.

They had come here, the white men, and taken her bones.

They had come here, the white men, and taken him out from under breast and wing.

This was what she felt like: a shot and dazed beast.

She had found this tongue-language in her sleep—someone did not want it.

She yelled out now, her hand up to her breast.

Then she saw it, the rising figure.

It was Gill.

The circumference of their bodies, one to another, hung in their speechlessness.

Sonny stepped forward. She wanted to say: Come here. Come to me.

Gill stood, his mouth ajar, and turned away from her.

The meeting, the earth around him, shook his face as he reached down for his gut and came to a shattering halt in the woods. The dragging of Curtis Willow crept behind him, near the shoulder blade: the oxygen of his territory was so suffocating that he eased his hand up to his face.

He moaned in his posture, as if drowning.

His lips parted, he began to breathe: his finger had left a streak of dirt on his cheek, and in the momentary division from his moaning, he had begun to smear it.

He set afoot, away from Sonny, who had long disappeared, and out into the opening where the sun had formed a blade over the Bullock house.

Lenora Bullock's mouth appeared, to some degree, as if it had been gouged of redemption. She stood in the diluted eye of a vertical mirror, her hand up to her thigh, her hip.

The same sharp line. The startling comparison of the dead, how the bone lies with a stiff, obligatory setting to the vertebrae.

She touched her thigh. Her entire hand rested there, her finger sliding into the crux of its position. Her belly, all pygmified, bellowed out from her ribs, as if it took no part in her ceremony.

It was no wonder that when she reached out for Hurry, he turned in his dreaming, away from the construction of her pale body: the doctor had told her, and she well knew it, that there was nothing to spare: a she bastard's deformity.

The wind from her nostrils seeped through her round head, the hairs parting.

For she had done nothing this morning, only stood in her wrinkled gown, facing an untied ribbon on her vanity, as if at any moment she would pull her hair up from her face and bridge the purpose of her activity to a close.

She had gotten word: the postmaster was out for good. Surgery. And now she would have to make the journey into town, go to the fabric store, and ask, her voice public, Anything good?

She could not bear it, although she was a part of the name—Bullock—and it was her post office and her town, her confined government. How it plagued her even more so now, the matter of her existence, how they'd all chatter and gossip about her.

Lenora Bullock. Orphan. The structure of the words pushed her chin outward, and there was no turning away from the mounted shape they'd formed in her head. Her index finger traveled up the pulse of her jugular, and she felt folded and laid aside like the battered fabric of an unwanted pattern, cut and fringed, asymmetrical.

She walked toward the vanity, the untied ribbon lying in wait, and pulled her hair up until the ribbon held its weight.

There was a knock at the door.

Disturbed, she faced the window. No horse.

She took her path down the staircase, and there she saw him, Gill.

Immediately, she traced the edge of the door's hinge: like Adam, he had stood in her kitchen, a boy on the eve of thirteen, and awaited the height of his measurement.

Of course she remembered him, could not forget the striking character of his shoulders: they were tyrannical, an output of in-credible power, manlike.

I come for Hurry, said Gill.

From his place, he stood with a thirst that seemed to gather in the hot and permeable heat around him.

Lenora Bullock stepped up to the screen, where his face had grown evermore solid in her mind. And with this, the memory of his folks—their abandonment of him—drew her eyelids together.

Gill, she whispered, how long now?

His hand traveled, without complexity, up to where her face was: it was not really her face that he saw but the darner needle that lay behind her, flat and elevated on a hooded sheet.

A white envelope lay beside it, the name ADAM.

Seasons, he said.

Well, don't let the heat take you, she said. Come in.

Gill stepped into the house, Lenora Bullock apologizing for her condition: her back turned now, she looked to him an unneces-sary depiction of vanity, her hair all tied up and pitiful, a train station baby.

How it had come down on him, how she'd made him stand near the door's edge in a vertical and wavering line, the moderate stench of her vagina throughout the air, as if she wanted him to stick his finger underneath her gown, find her freedom.

She poured him a glass of lemonade and motioned for him to join her at the kitchen table. Hurry's out, she said. The morgue.

An invisible corpse seemed to lie between them: Gill, at the audible news of *the morgue*, could hear the sound of both pulley and laughter. The nigger. The nigger is dead. He heard it and then, too, saw the broken ankle of the foot. It dangled from the chain, the circular bone out of proportion, bloody.

What time's he due? he asked.

Not sure, said Lenora Bullock.

In her response, she turned toward the costume she had made for Adam. It hung on the curtain rod above the windowsill. She wanted to show him, just now, what she had done, the meticulous embroidering of the hooded Klan suit: she hoped, if only for the value of her breathing, that he would come to notice.

It wrung in his head like the time he'd seen an accordion player stumble in front of him, his foot out of step, the sound of the instrument disappearing underneath the tracks of the railroad deck, the final tune muted and catastrophic.

Thirsty, ain't you? she asked.

Gill picked up the glass she had prepared and drank her lemonade, the Klan suit rising in the wind of heat. He then stood to his feet: Tell 'm I come.

Lenora Bullock stepped toward him.

Never said what you turned into, she commented.

Her head broke the alignment of her body.

He faced her as if he knew it would hurt: A clerk, he whispered. The railroad.

His response forced her fingers apart. She reached behind her for the arm of a chair. It alone held the ingredients of her memory together.

For Gill had stepped away from the porch, his head a blur.

chapter
fifteen

Adam lay in the dust, the moon perpendicular like the panting iris of a victim.

The entire globe hung above him, white and circular.

There on the powdered ground, he opened the shape of his mouth and let it hang there—the shape—the oxygen bleeding into a cloud.

He was on his stomach, Midnight beside him, listening to the Bullocks and his father in the barn. They breathed with a sort of agony, loud and wet, the atmospheric pressure of their bodies rising upward.

The Klan suit hung from a cowhided loop above their figures. And so it was done: the pale fabric of the thing that had been sewn together was cause enough for their laughter. How they looked at it: the crooked details of the hemline, stitched and punctured by the darner needle of Lenora Bullock's ripe, ill-fated measurement.

D. D. Pickens stepped out onto the breakfast porch. Adam yet lay in the dust as she journeyed toward him. Adam, she said. You're dirty.

At the sound of her voice, he turned.

I know, he said.

His hand went up to his forehead and it would not go away, the laughter of his father and the Bullocks, the Klan suit, the humidity of the earth and moon, at once and altogether striking.

D. D. Pickens was lake fog. She had come from the house white and out of place in her mockingbird bone. It was her lurking, her inability to disturb the meeting, to extract the feeding tube from her speech, that made it all the more seem that she had nowhere to put it.

A buzzing mosquito fluttered in the space around her. The turbulence of the wings, tactile and disobedient, was electrifying. As the hummingbird, it had come to find her, as if she had called upon it. She stretched out her hand. It roared on the bridge of her elongated arm and bit her.

She turned toward the laughter of the barn. They were invisible and naked, a cylindrical cone inside her head. A nigger. A bird: the difference exploded and swiveled in her head, down the cylindrical cone and upon the item of her thinking, and she could not hold herself together on purpose.

Her arm fell to her side. She went back into the house before pausing on the steps of the breakfast porch. Go to your father, she whispered.

Midnight panted around her, the odor of his tongue permanent: he caught the tail end of her gown. It was not out of malice, but as if to say, We don't want to be here.

Her face remained hidden until she forced the fabric out of his jaw—the gown torn—and disappeared into the dull seed of the house.

Adam lifted himself from the dust, a pain in his backbone from lying down so long a time, and faced the barn. Hoover Pickens signaled to him, the Bullocks behind him like a sharp and heavy jade: the moon had forced their yellow bodies into the alignment of disaster.

Adam, yelled Hoover Pickens, get yonder.

Midnight had come to a halt before the men. Hurry Bullock stepped out of the horizontal line. There fell a discernible silence: the panting had drawn him forward. He was mesmerized by the manner in which the pulse of Midnight's breathing had pushed his belly out.

There lived within Hurry Bullock a fascination with the dead. Now, in his potent and deliberate nature, he had stopped the breathing of this animal. He had laid him upon the table at the morgue and come down, down upon the breathing organ, caused it to burst.

He had done it in his mind.

Midnight walked backward, away from Hurry Bullock and the men, until he felt the security of Adam behind him.

What's a matter, boy? asked Adam.

The hairs of Midnight's spine stood upward, the resistance of gravity.

Hoover Pickens broke the silence again: Son, get yonder.

Adam looked up at Hurry Bullock, who stood in his place, a grin about him that lifted the defining muscle of his jawbone. Even in the light of the moon, Adam could see how far-reaching it was. He had seen Hurry Bullock from his window, the malignancy of his standing. He looked then, as now, a resounding tumor.

He walked between the men, his chin upward to the hanging Klan suit.

Salem, the brother of Hurry Bullock, stood beside him.

Adam's father reached for his shoulder: Son, he said. It's done went through.

The men rejoined themselves in laughter. The commandments of the Bullock Klan hung there, too, up high above the stable of horses and men: it had all come forward, the corpse he had witnessed in Hurry Bullock's morgue, the contents of the dead man's pocket, the emptying of his stomach.

Bring it down! yelled Hurry Bullock.

The Bullocks had begun to clap, each man in his own recanting sound, as Hoover Pickens walked toward a battered nail and tugged at a rope line connected to the pulley. The hooded Klan suit began to come down.

It was the color of opium.

The horses reared in an uproar.

Adam alone heard the solitary, disturbing chaos like the final tune of a tumbling accordion.

Go, son, said Hoover Pickens. Try it on.

There was a push to his shoulders.

The men redeemed their clapping. The sweat, the mixture of sound and hurry, all a devouring edge of false, sanctimonious outrage that bellowed like a fiery and struck cloud of smoke: it shifted the bones of the throat to suffocation.

Take to it, son.

Adam paused.

A voice, at once familiar, rose from the crowd.

I come to help, whispered Gill.

The men paused.

Hurry Bullock stepped out with his foot, circling Gill with rhythmic mobility: the same sporadic design of the jawline, vast and angular now. There was no sign of expression. So nude and jarring was the presence of Gill that it seemed never to belong to pity.

Gill stood in his gaze: he thought of how his father had walked him through the woods to the Bullock house for training. The heated sun was beaten into his father's wrist, the winding print of a wrenlike pattern traveling toward the palm, as if an egg had been hatched.

You hear that, boys? yelled Hurry Bullock. He's come to help.

For a moment, silence seeped into the wind of Gill's disturbance, but then it broke and the men surrounded him. It was good that he had come.

Hoover Pickens signaled for Adam.

Adam stepped forward. He shook with the memory of the encounter.

The words: You never saw me.

With this, he realized the power of his own pretending.

Adam, said Hoover Pickens. This here's Gill Mender.

Gill faced Adam: Couldn't help but hear, he said. You're the talk o' the station.

Salem Bullock patted Gill on the shoulder: the weight of his hand was judicious, a kind of burdensome tremor that pushed the root of Gill's sleeve into a pouch. The air had come out of his shirt, the odor of solitude.

Gill abandoned Adam, the men, and stood before the hooded Klan suit. He waited for it, but no one, not even Hurry Bullock, questioned where he had been all this time. Again he was amid the dragging season.

He lifted the fabric from its place and put his face in it. Hate carried within it the ageless stench of the corpse: it lived beneath his eyelid, Curtis Willow.

Adam, he said. Come to.

Midnight had begun to howl. This was when Adam joined Gill.

And it was Gill who led the men in the reciting of the commandment:

> *We are white men, born unto the earth*
> *And land, which is ours and belongs to us, as*
> *Free and automatic white men.*
> *All niggers must be obedient.*
> *They are not a part of the human thread,*
> *But are animals and must be dragged from*
> *Their properties and stricken from the*
> *Blood of the nation.*
> *The same thing goes for hypocrites.*

Gill brought the hooded Klan suit upon Adam's head and, amid the chaos, whispered: I come to help.

chapter
sixteen

There fell within the context of her body an obesity drawn about her so that it bulged over the blade of her shoulder, a redness throughout her face; the heat had swelled in her stomach. She had begun to sweat, her yellow hair singed like the healing effects of a bruise.

She waited at the train station, alongside a row of others in their wait: beside her, a child with little connection to the breast he had woken from dangled on the edge of an elongated wooden chair. His mouth hung low. As it happened, he had discovered how warm it was coming out: a stream of urine had come out of his penis and now leaked from under him, from the seat of the wooden chair onto the floor, as if all along he had planned its journey.

A grin, somewhat cunning in its cruelty, trapped the contours of his round head, and he pointed to it, the urine, and his tiny shoulders began to rise in the warmth of the disaster he had created. Look, he said.

The woman who held him, who had just released him from her breast, heard the malicious gathering in his throat, the manner in which he had used the word *look*, and in her embarrassment of what he had done, the urine all about, she slapped his face.

Everyone heard it, even the sleeping and dilapidated man who had once dropped his accordion—a tumbling that had cost him sound—and saw, with amazement, how the child turned to the woman and, too, slapped her square-shaped head into vision.

She brought her hand up to her face, a hue of scarlet on her cheek, and picked up the child by his arm and stripped him until all at once he stood in his nudity, his penis holding a steady and crooked vein where it seemed to predict the ferocity of his exposure.

The obese woman could not hold in her sitting. The sun struck the horizontal window of the train station and landed on her calf: she wore a sandal, strapped at the toe; the oval muscle of her foot, near the swollen ankle, bore the resemblance of an embryo—plucked from the belly of a dirty syringe, jelly-like.

They were all waiting for Gill: the man who had tumbled in his steps and dropped his accordion, the woman and the nude child, the others who waited with deafening activity for a ticket. All except the obese woman, now pregnant: she pretended—her posture told of it—that someone was coming to get her, a man from Bullock, perhaps. If only she waited, he *would* come and she could get out of these clothes and rest her vertebrae, the pressure of baby weight pinning her to one side.

Indeed, a man from Bullock opened the door of the train station, a bell sounding. Her eyes, once drawn to her sunlit ankle, leaned in to a solitary, muted gaze, when she lifted her shoulders, as if to say, Come for me?

But the man, gray-haired and linear, lifted the sleeve of his shirt to track the hour of his standing and, while in his place, nothing else to capture his attention, let go of a sigh that had taken too long a time to come out—heat, he supposed—looked at the obese woman and she heard it: Too fat.

He wore a hat upon his molecular head, a feather extended above his forehead from a mahogany-colored band at its center. The nude child began to sob. The mother laid him on the fabric of her lap, and his body shook in the rising temperature of the horizontal window.

Not even the nerve to love him, he thought.

The mother of the nude child stared at the awkward and jutted setting of the feathered cap, the odor of urine bleeding into the saturated clothing beside her. She had seen him before, perhaps in Memphis, the train's final destination. He was as poised as ever and attuned with the same judgment of the things he had witnessed, as if he were greater than the perplexities of the world, and nothing—not even fire—could bid him compassion.

Without word, he nodded at her.

She had seen how he looked at the obese woman and turned toward her, the determinable signs of an orphan abounding in her pitiful face as she drew her head forward. Her hair, travel-beaten and distorted in color, fell around her ears, a part through the center.

The nude child had fallen asleep.

It *was* Memphis where she had seen him. It was he, the accordion seller, who had taken the train from Bullock each Monday afternoon and sat on the little bench outside the Memphis ticket counter telling of the quality of the instrument: each accordion had a note in it, a message for the mute.

The man whose accordion had tumbled underneath the train's coming stood to greet the accordion seller. He had no speech. His larynx had been crushed under the weight of a cog wheel: the reins of the mule had come loose from his father's grip, a sudden jolting of the wagon, and thus it happened, the crumbling of the bones.

He took from his pocket a bound journal of his writings, until he reached a quiet page, ivory-like, and jotted down the language of his questioning.

The accordion seller awaited the first line.

Will work for it, these were the beginning words.

The accordion seller lacked expression.

The man without sound wrote a second line. The jotting down of the words leaked throughout the train station among the waiters, carbon monoxide.

Old one dead was the second line.

The accordion seller laughed at the muted man, as if he had become aware, in his matter-of-fact overture, that he was God. Such is life, he said.

The man without sound tapped the dull edge of the stencil on the page. He remained with what he had written the second time: *Old one dead.*

The accordion seller looked down at the tie he was wearing and reached for the knot he had made this morning. He loosened it with an arrogance about him that rose above the horizontal window, the obese woman, and the nude child; he wanted them to see how far he'd made it.

He wanted them to beg.

The man without sound wrote a third line in his journal: *Have mercy.*

No one could depict how the man had come from such humility. Even the obese woman thought in her mind how she had not the symptoms of begging, when it did not at all matter: she, too, was without speech.

The accordion seller flipped his hand at the man without sound and turned to face the door he had come out of, the bell halted in its chiming. Heavy, ain't it? he whispered.

The man without sound heard it. So did they all. They heard it and in their collective waiting wanted the accordion seller to burn in this heat.

If only he would stand near the horizontal window, right up to the face of it, so the sun, in its fiery and catastrophic temperature, could set him ablaze.

The bell rang at the accordion seller's near departure, and Gill, accompanied by Adam, met him where he stood.

Mr. Satchell, said Gill.

The accordion seller nodded. Train's late, he said.

Gill walked past the accordion seller and into the ticket booth. An oval-shaped hole for the waiting customers to lean their mouths into.

Immediately, the waiters formed a line before him.

Adam, he said. Wait there.

Adam stood near the obese woman, an empty seat beside her. The humidity had risen in her face, her arms in front of her like the trembling meekness of agony.

He took his place.

The woman shook the nude child out of his sleep, and he reached for her breast to hold his discomfort. She patted him on the spine with a territorial forgiveness. He was the bait of her existence.

She had sat here, as did the accordion seller, every Monday afternoon awaiting the train to Memphis: the nude child had succumbed to a raging ear infection. She had heard of the doctor at the end of the railroad; he would pay for the expense of travel, give free medicine and coupons for penetration.

She knew, even in her waiting, that she was powerless.

The man without sound was near the wooden railing that separated the ticket holder from the train's coming. I could do it now. No one to grab hold, he thought. Jump.

The obese woman and Adam singularly looked out at him. The obese woman, in her terror, lifted her swollen hand in midair for a moment, but he had walked away from the railing, the journal tucked inside his pocket.

Memphis, said Gill. One by one, they took their tickets and stepped out of the train station and onto the wooden plank outside of the horizontal window.

The bulb of the obese woman's ankle was stained. The sun had crawled right up her calf and singed it.

Everyone had begun to clear out of the train station.

Gill wore a cap with two yellow lines on it. He removed it from his head and looked down at the blazer he had worn this afternoon. And up thereafter to the obese woman beside Adam.

When he saw such women in their waiting, he could not help but think of his own pitiful mother and her abandonment of him, the scent of the orphanage in the milk of her breasts, the stone he had swallowed—he approached the obese woman.

She looked up at him, down toward her heated foot.

Nobody's coming, said Gill.

There was an indication in his speech, a penetrable explosion of telepathy.

She was exposed.

Go home, said Gill.

The obese woman ran out and away from the silent train station, the things she had seen—the accordion seller and the muted man, the nude child—and onto the wooden plank where the ticket dwellers were and drew herself to a pause near the railing where she had only moments before risen her swollen hand in an effort to avert the catastrophe of the muted man and thought of it: Jump.

But the accordion seller, in his need for idolatry, took her by the arm and, in their disappearance, patted her hair down; in her hurry, it had flung out of category from her large head.

Adam, said Gill, the train's coming.

Gill Mender had no more in his words given instruction to Adam than D. D. Pickens when she walked through the wooded forest and gathered Midnight in her arms to heal him. She simply wanted him to breathe.

Adam, in his naïveté, took to Gill, followed him throughout the course of his footsteps with gaping thirst. A journey had begun to develop between them that caused him to sit up from his covers: his father had hung it there above his window, the hooded Klan suit. He was learning what the matter was.

The train had come to a complete stop at the railing. Gill stood near the machine until a Negro porter stepped down from the opening.

Gill looked at him and nodded.

Adam stood inside the train station.

The Negro porter walked toward the horizontal window; the door opened.

Adam had never been so close, had only seen the rigor mortis of the corpse in Hurry Bullock's morgue. This was how the living eye moved: the gait of the body before hooked to the pulley, bloody.

Now, only he and the Negro porter stood in the waiting area of the train station.

The Negro porter paused at the sight of him: he stood with proportionate symmetry to the chair that had held the obese woman's weight. The train talk had been beaten into the contours of his face, a sort of inconsiderate erosion that caused his head to lean forward. Adam had seen this in horses, the inability of the spine to resist.

Adam, the sun bleeding around him, stepped toward the Negro porter, who stood and waited for him without any sign of collision.

The Negro porter, whose round and unbatted eye began to water let Adam touch him: Adam had begun to trace the edges of the Negro porter's eyelid and, in a moment of silence, opened the palm of his hand and covered the entire sphere of his dark and roaming eye. He felt it: the closing of the globe, how it pulsated on the edge of his hand, as if to steady the reasoning behind the encounter.

The ringing of the bell had long stopped.

Adam's hand traveled to the mouth, ajar and whispering, up to the flaring nostrils.

Without difference, he had remembered the bird he had trapped in the barn, his tiny fingers over the entire face, the beak warm and perfect.

The train whistle blew.

The conductor stepped away from the machine and, in his urgency, swung open the door to the train station: Adam pulled his hand away from the Negro porter's face with electrifying hurry.

Nigger, yelled the conductor. The luggage.

Yes, sir, said the Negro porter. Yes, sir.

The yelling, the niggers, the train talk, leaked into Adam's eardrum.

The conductor awaited the Negro porter—who had disappeared behind the ticket counter—looked at Adam, and nodded.

Adam stepped backward, his hand up to his face, and away from the horizontal window where Gill stood on the wooden plank.

The Negro porter grabbed the luggage and was aboard the train. He hung from a vertical post on the machine as the train began to whistle a third time.

He put his hand up to his face and kept it there until the train took to its tracks and the meeting between them went down in the umbilical heat of dust and cloud.

Gill walked inside the train station, picked up the urine-sodden clothes of the nude child—past the obese woman's sitting chair, the lone page abandoned by the muted man that lay battered on the wooden floor—and through the back doors of the train station, and tossed them into the Mississippi.

Adam, he yelled. Let's go.

Adam, yet hung by the atmospheric pressure of the Negro porter's face, looked down at the palm of his hand, and there it was, the print of a beak, a bird.

chapter seventeen

D. D. Pickens woke alone.

She lay on the pillows, a pounding beneath her cheekbone. She touched it, her fingers suffocating the nerve. Suddenly, in the hallucinatory setting of her head, she had been looked upon from the window—an element of her own creation—and wished for it, whatever it was, to strike a crashing blow across her face.

She looked beside her, blood.

A cough steered Hoover Pickens out of his sleep by morning. He would wake as if flung from a beast—his hand the only source of gravity—and out of the moon's eye. He stuck his hand down his throat. He wanted all of it, at one time, to come out of him. And even in his pleading did his lung refuse to obey him.

The lung held it, a seeping hole in the organ, an aching explosion.

D. D. Pickens pretended not to have heard it: she lay on her side upon his return, had practiced the rhythm of her sleeping as though to avoid the depiction of agony.

She could not think of it, would rather have been struck across the face with death, perhaps, rather than carry on like . . . like the woman in the fabric store. How many years now her husband had been dead. She remembered the bullet, through the cranium it went, a hole in his head.

As she lay, she thought of the months following his death, how the woman at the fabric store, the widow, had walked to the edge of the steps, a carelessness about her: the remnant of possession.

The widow had come down from the steps of the fabric store and, in her yawning, broke the surface of a spun web that had lived for a time between the space of two vertical columns. When she recognized the thing of which she had done, she left her arm out in public: the spider, in its nomadic pattern, crawled up the base of her arm, near the shoulder.

She reached for it. Her opposite hand and finger came down, close to the blade where the spider had attached itself to her palm. She looked out at D. D. Pickens and, with or without the need for attention, brought her hands together and she cared not who saw it: the spider was dead.

D. D. Pickens watched as the widow took her hand and mounted the corpse on the tip of her index finger. And ate it.

Were it not for Adam's sickness, D. D. Pickens never would have witnessed this.

A maliciousness about the widow, fixed isolation, perhaps, plunged from the stability of her ego and into the burning hemisphere of heat around her. No wonder they found him dead: her husband all bloated and fat on the covers, the wound leaking from his lips, the mouth bruised by fascination, a bullet.

The widow made her sick. Her will for independence. If killing was an announcement, the manner of her introduction to the world that she was, at last, here, then must she pass it down the line, the throat?

D. D. Pickens lived alongside the muscle of a narrow corridor. It was as narrow as her mind. She had to be told, had only moved

to the diction of her very own Hoover Pickens, who bade her attention no more than the source of his waking.

The blood that woke Hoover was dark now. There lay a threaded
seam from the pillows and onto the floor—she could measure with
proximity the exact manner of which he reached for his belly, the
position he had conformed to in his sickness. Near the pulse of
the sunlit window was where his arm rose above his head, a fever.
And there was where he tried to hold it, the drum, the cough. Her
own blood had come to a close without him.

The blade of her confinement muted.

He was not dead, but she felt it, dreamed of the happening. He
would wake from the bed, reach out in front of him, and stumble,
lie there with his lips parted: a stream of blood from his lung oozing out, away from the tongue.

She imagined, too, how the widow had done it: her husband
had been sick, a disease, and had finally drifted into the rhythm
of a coma. Everyone had heard about it, how the doctor had gone
out to the widow's house and willed her husband dead. He had
been lifted from the covers, frozen with rigor mortis, and onto a
wooden gurney. He lay as they found him, in the fetal position.

D. D. Pickens, now more than ever a time, saw the widow in
her gown, the gun in her hands, and heard the final blow, the blast
of gunpowder from behind: a bullet to the back of the head blasts
the cells out of equilibrium. The shoulder grows heavy, cannot
account for the loss of weight, and the torso leans in to the catastrophe, and whether sitting or lying down, it looks as though it
has been pushed from the spine on purpose.

Now she forced the pillow out of proportion and brought it to
her: a wrinkle, trapped by the pattern of her husband's breathing,
shaped itself into the fabric. Her fingertip caught it, smoothed it
out of perplexity.

Had anyone been in the house at this moment, he would not have heard it. She moaned from her stomach and into the hem where the blood was. She thought of Adam at birth, the vulnerability of his round head. She had lain down next to him, her hand over the fontanel—a pulse there, the skull without bone—as if the exposure of the cranium struck the testimony of her solitude: she shook so when she thought of it.

The morning of Adam's conception, she had emerged nude from her bathing, her hair and body wet, and stood near the edge of the window. She was drawn to the chimera of a lighted star, her full eye upward. It was without benefit that she did not hear him.

Hoover Pickens stood behind her, penis erect. What do you want? he asked.

At this particular and yet pitiful moment, she turned only a little to say to him, Look at it, when he plunged his penis into her. She could remember now the aching of her collarbone: the tapping, tapping of the shoulder, until at once, a cracked fissure drew itself upon the glass window, a tiny sound and, suddenly, mute.

The coming of Adam.

Was it hate that she had felt when, indeed, it was Hoover Pickens who had taken her in, a dirty stone, and brought her here to live and be his, belong to him? Perhaps it *was* gratitude that caused her to neglect how he smothered the pounding muscle in her face so that now she could feel it, even in her hummingbird bone, throb within the mobility of her cheek.

D. D. Pickens was not vindictive: she held neither the gall nor the appetite for holding a gun, as she had not the courage to swallow a spider. Her stomach, so hungry it was for shelter that she simply turned from the cracked window and drew her breath in so as to blame it all on the world and slipped beneath the covers.

By morning, none of it had happened.

A dream.

They hung on one line: she, Adam, and Hoover Pickens. Drawn out in her mind with one stroke. She had not paid attention, but her hand trembled the entire time. The line was as crooked and distorted as the spine pushed by the tip of the finger.

Someone entered the house.

She stood for a moment, silence.

D. D., yelled Lenora Bullock, get down yonder. I've got pie.

The voice of Lenora Bullock, familiar and disturbing, caused her to abandon the pillow. A microscopic surge of light fell through the eye of the window and disappeared through an opening on the wooden floor.

It had gone down below, down to the axis of Lenora Bullock's full arm: she discovered it in rotation, her wrist upturned. The parallel beam of light sat on the vein. Through the course of its pulsation, her free hand fell to her hip. She measured the synchronicity of wrist to hip, both with pounding texture: her jaw-bone had fallen out of the alignment of her mouth as she stood in her remote discovery.

The sound of D. D. Pickens traveling down the stairs of the house flung her arm out of position.

D. D. Pickens's hair hung at the shoulder. The warmth of the parallel beam of light had sunk into the globe of her eye. She had stepped into it.

I done brought pie, said Lenora Bullock, her powdered birth-mark annihilated from the things of the room.

They had both seen the parallel beam of light, equally and with hesitation, an extraordinary pulling, a magnet.

D. D. Pickens opened the kitchen drawer, took up a knife, and joined Lenora Bullock, who sat at the table with her hands in front of her.

Salem's done sick, said Lenora Bullock.

D. D. Pickens brought the pie toward her and cut it. What's took 'm?

Lenora Bullock looked down at her wrist, still burning: Spitting up blood.

Lenora shouldn't have come today, thought D. D. Pickens. Of all the times Lenora Bullock had brought news into her house: she noticed the downward slope of her eyelid, the whole matter of her speech narcissistic, as if it were unbearable for her to think and breathe and be one person.

I say he's spitting up blood, repeated Lenora Bullock. Weak, I reckon.

Lenora had set the table. Two forks. Two plates. The patterns of their arrangement were forced into condition.

D. D. Pickens sat the pie before her, her plate empty.

Leaves a stain, said Lenora Bullock.

Something of preservation rose between the two women, belonging more to Lenora Bullock. Her voice, trained to exaggeration, erupted out of an invisible fascination with pity. A stone.

Blood, she whispered.

The words, entrapment.

A hole punctured Lenora Bullock beneath her breasts, the entire abdomen failing to participate in her exhalation: D. D. Pickens had done it. She had begun to ask herself why Lenora Bullock had come here this morning.

And so Lenora Bullock had eaten her slice, conformed to the spine of her chair, and looked out at the empty plate. The parallel beam lay between her and D. D. Pickens, and there could be seen the sperm of floating molecules. Dust.

You hadn't touched it, D. D., she said. Seems you done had a slice by now, all the time it took.

Not hungry, whispered D. D. Pickens.

Without comment, Lenora Bullock rose from her chair.

A photo of irritation, mockery.

She knew not what she had done. But could only think to say it again without regard to how loud and pregnant it was: weak.

Her hand traveled from her hip and into the dust of the parallel beam of light. After all she had done, the sewing of the robe, to be treated with such despondency.

Her finger struck the molecular dust.

Sonny Willow had begun to howl in the woods.

D. D. Pickens stood up to face Lenora Bullock: Leaves a stain, she whispered.

Lenora Bullock, in turn, walked away from the Pickens house, the bed of her wrist burning.

chapter
eighteen

The rain made him cold.

Gill Mender had run through it, trembling.

Five years he had lived in the abandoned house: everything in one room.

The rain spun around him and he knew how a part of the spinning he was when it came to him: Curtis Willow. Come out, nigger.

He had said it, his very own mouth: Curtis's head was dirty, the debris of the dragging woven into it, the skull cracked as if the blade of a shovel had gone down into it and a man, any man, had stuck his foot on the edge of it and pushed down on it, so he would go ahead and do his swelling where he was, that way the blood'd burst right out of him and onto the ground. But they—the Bullock Klansmen—made *him* do it.

Come here, son, they said. Push down on it.

No, sir. Gill whispered. Don't make me.

But Hurry Bullock snatched him out of his begging and lit a match where the head was and made him put his foot on the shovel and jump down on it. That *was* how his eye popped out: the pressure of the blade pushed his brains forward—near the nostril— not enough room in the socket.

When a nigger's head bursts, the earth takes him inward, into her bosom, and she washes the blood out of his hair, straightens his foot out, and she cannot bear to see him as she found him, all broken up like that, and patches his head together. Mud.

The large and blurry window, adjacent to Gill's standing, held the smear of his fingerprint, and as he stood in the room, alone and without, he recalled the energy of the house after the dragging: his father had walked up behind him, patted him on the shoulder of his right arm. A mixture of rain and dirt had run down the sodden sleeve of his robe, onto the brink of his index finger, the floor.

What had he done? The howling of Curtis Willow drifted down his throat. He swallowed, his hand up to the window. Rain-dirt.

Good boy, son, whispered his father.

Not only his father but all of the Klansmen were in the one-room house: Hoover Pickens and the Bullocks—the husband of the widow—stood around him with an air of diversion about them. Even his mother.

Hear how that nigger called out? said one of the men. We put him down. We put him down.

Their laughter rose with expansion, darted throughout their conversation like the arrogance of light in the wrong eye: The nigger, the nigger, hear how he called out? they yelled. For mercy.

No one had noticed: a brown recluse spider crawled atop the hood of the widow's husband. Gill had seen it—a thing of powerful solidarity—leap down from a singular, webbed line and onto his Klan suit.

Dead nigger now, he yelled.

Among the words *Dead nigger now*, the brown recluse crept upon him, near the skull, as if both line and activity carried the same result. He laughed and his throat held it. The spider paused.

Jungle blood, said Hurry Bullock.

Again the laughter consumed them.

He hollered, that one, said the widow's husband. A kite.

They held on to the master Klansman's tale, the grandfather of Hurry and Salem Bullock: an embroidered kite had flown above his house like a bird, stirred by wind and earth. It had begun to whistle. The sound, how it drew him to anger—a nigger to a white woman—a nigger's head was what he imagined as he reached for his gun. Shot it down.

Gill's father stood from his chair. Wild and on purpose, he brought his shoulders forward and, with imitation, opened his mouth, ape-like. The primordial sound hung in the echo of the pregnant house. Each of them yelling, Jungle blood, jungle blood.

We put him down. We put him down.

None of them was aware. The noise, the yelling out, moved the spider out of position, upward and onto the spine of the widow's husband, up to the cranium. It sat there a moment upon the yellow hairs of his head.

The pouch of the spider's belly, woven from some sort of restlessness, seemed at once deflated, the poison rushing through.

The widow's husband halted in his laughter as his finger traveled upward to the skull. His head had begun to itch. The spider disappeared beyond the hairs of his head, and Gill saw that it departed, as it had come, down the fabric of the hood and onto the singular webbed line strung from the tiny opening in the ceiling.

I taught 'm good, said Hurry Bullock.

Gill stood at the center of the table. They gazed upon him.

His mother, in her obscure manner, reached into her pocket. Prior to the dragging, her letter had come from the Vital Life Office. Her father had been found. Somewhere in Tennessee.

She, too, bore the stain of a birthmark: it lay hidden beneath the bulb of her breast, the agonizing age of primacy.

She had shared the news with only Gill's father: how could she take Gill with them, the predicament of her own weight a germ to carry?

So much happens when two people lie down together. They whisper, one to another, among themselves, as if the secret of their morbidity will spill out, rise from the cloud of their breathing and into the next bed where the boy sleeps, his eardrum battered with it all the while.

Their love was impenetrable.

For Gill knew: he had never fully been included.

Of course he had heard them. They would leave in the early morning, abandon him while he slumbered. His mother would kiss him on the mouth, so as to leave him with the scent of her milk. And journey with his father to the train station for Tennessee.

Indeed, she knelt down beside his bed the following morning, his father behind her, and kissed him. After the closing of the door, he ran to the window, watched them go.

The sour odor of the men, his father, yet lingered. He looked down at his misshapen hands. He would do this at night, too. The moon lighted upon them, a course of interdependency. Man and evolution.

Midnight had begun to bark.

Gill opened the door and stepped out onto the porch. He had drawn a map for Adam. I want to show you something, he commented. They had been sitting amid the Pickenses when he said it. Adam's hand went up to his face, a grin seeped through.

Adam ran through the downpour of the forest, Midnight following, until Gill bade him to safety.

You done come, said Gill. Follow me.

They disappeared behind the house—both the hue of milk spewing out—and up toward the barn: with distinct and utter separation, it was atop the hill.

The doors had been barred with a single wooden board.

Wait here, yelled Gill.

He returned with a hammer and pried it loose.

The rain blew down upon him and he looked out, out into the woods with desperation: he could have lain in it right now, he thought, opened his mouth, and let it through.

Midnight and Adam were inside the barn now.

Gill, the last to go through, closed the door behind them and walked toward a lantern, struck a match that had lain beside it, and, at once, lit the wick.

There seemed a fog throughout the entire place, the flame rising upward, up toward the haystacks, bale by bale, that shifted above them, all out of line and link with symmetry: Gill had placed them this way out of purpose, pulled them away from the land of an adjacent field, only the moon-face above him.

Midnight panted and, in this light, his head a crowbar, turned sideways. For a short while, his belly protruded outward, away from the earth, as if at any moment he'd come undone, a tug of the tail, a strand to unweave.

Gill stood apart from Adam, his weight supported by the heel of his foot.

Adam looked down at the lantern: it hung from Gill's hand, had set the bones of the wrist into an equation, a dangerous independence, so that he pictured it, the fumes spreading throughout, up to the shoulder, the entire head ablaze.

Midnight stretched his hind legs, a yawn came from him, and he lay down on a lone bale of hay, his tongue bellowing out.

Gill stepped forward and paused: I gotta show you some'n.

Adam followed him.

Gill remembered, in his naive and candid footsteps, how he had trailed Hurry Bullock, how he had wanted to pull Hurry Bullock's pistol out of his pocket, put it up to his head, near the temple, and . . . he envisioned it, a tiny hole traveling through one side of the head and coming out, a blow to the skull: in his childish and weary mind, he had assumed it would look like a red dot above the ear, shift the head a little and he'd fall to the ground, look like he'd been sleeping all the time.

Gill reached out behind him, passing the lantern to Adam. Hold it, he whispered.

They had come to a vast wooden gate in the barn: a horse approached.

If Adam had ever seen such a creature, such a testimony of strength and moment, he could not think of it. The horse breathed from the nostrils, a stirring of the eye away from him and Gill and back toward them. A pink cloud lived around the globe of his pupils. He was pale in color, bone-white.

Adam walked up toward him, his hand over the horse's face. He had not yet touched him before Gill interrupted: How come you don't ride none? he asked.

Used to, whispered Adam.

How come you don't now?

Fell, said Adam, the horse stirring in its steps.

Go ahead, said Gill. Touch 'm.

Adam walked beside the horse, his hand on the belly. The sincerity of the creature's breathing, the pausing of the gut, drew him to breathe and pause in the same obedient pattern.

What's his name? asked Adam.

Blade.

Gill's response hung in the fog around them. Adam, asked Gill, you fell one time? You fell one time 'n' you quit?

Adam nodded.

Then you ain't been taught? asked Gill.

Yeah, whispered Adam. I done been taught.

By who?

Mr. Hurry, said Adam.

The name hung in Gill's head, and he held his ribs together as it occurred to him what he must do and what the boy, Adam, must do to save them both.

He could not bear to think of it: Adam's round head seemed altogether vulnerable to the language, the men who'd sit at his table in their Klan suits and Klan talk and mimic, laugh about a thing so pitiful as murder and jungle blood, and his mother, D. D. Pickens, with her unreachable polarity, would just stand there— with the rest of them—and leave him sobbing in the window, only the stain of a kiss holding him together.

Adam, he whispered. There's something you gotta do.

Gill whirled in his standing. He wanted to sit down, but there was nothing there to catch him. Adam, you've gotta take to Blade. He's gotta catch wind o' your scent. There's something . . . There's something you gotta do.

The final blow of the sentence he had murmured seemed to spin him out of natural proportion, and he hoped his gut would keep and the laughter of the Bullocks and Hoover Pickens, his mother's abandonment, would leave his heart tidy and without restlessness. But he knew none of that would ever happen, not as long as he had not corrected the horrible thing he had done, the calling out of Curtis Willow.

It was as if he had invited it, Come in, Come in, but he had not at all invited the words. They had come without invitation and stung him, a swarm of bees, in his liver and his full mind, and he realized how the accordion player must have felt without his music there to keep him safe. The raging sound of the last tune consumed him, the accidental hurling of the instrument crushed by the machine, the accordion player wailing behind it. He had come so close, held it for a temporary and depleted time, before the silence of the muted tune struck him—defeated—and the moisture drifted apart from the eyelid and so suddenly did it strike him, a widow.

Adam's hand rested on the muscle of the horse's rib. He paused: What's I gotta do, Gill?

But Gill had gone from the gate, away from the horse and Adam.

Adam left the horse and walked through the fog of the barn.

Gill's figure appeared. He was sitting on a haystack, his head between his knees.

His hand disappeared from his position: he had reached for his eardrum to muzzle it, the words and their degradation, and his arm went down behind him: he had not realized it then. This was the forced position of Curtis Willow, his arms tied behind him where he could not even reach out of the morbidity of his screaming to grab hold of his face, the pain, the pain seeping through.

Gill, asked Adam. What's I gotta do?

Gill reached out his hand and whispered and hoped Adam would hear it this one time, so the agony of holding himself in one piece would not leak out: You gotta take to Blade. You gotta ride 'm like you belong to 'm.

Adam paused.

Blade's sick and I'm sick and you've got some sick comin' to you . . . and I . . . I get a fever so just keepin' it, he said.

Midnight rose from his side. He ran up to and away from Adam, and when he saw it, he gnashed his teeth together and up toward it—Adam, too, saw it—there hung above Gill's discomfort, a Klan suit.

It had announced itself through the fog, bloody.

It looked and was shaped like his own. Lenora Bullock's doing, a darner needle. The pale-turned-bloody fabric shifted in the air of the barn, strung from the hook of a pulley.

Gill, he murmured, Midnight at his side. I'll take to 'm.

Gill rose out of his perplexity and joined him, both returning to the stall where a singular and sporadic drop of rain had crawled through the loose seam of the rooftop and down onto the pink cloud of Blade's round and indelible eye.

chapter nineteen

Three days now, the rain had gone on so.

Emma New had come out of the Thomas house. Lung wind pushed her lips apart. She let her hair down to plait it: her fingers had gone up, up to her head, where she discovered a webbed line strung from the center. She stepped right into it, a web.

She took it between the space of her tiny hand. She left her fingers apart until the buzzing, a blowfly, perched itself upon the line that had now become a limb of rest.

A blowfly. The insect of the dead. The lavender head, the bulging eye. The buzzing, the buzzing of Curtis Willow. After they took Curtis Willow up into the wheelbarrow, the insects perched on the blood and buzzed, buzzed throughout the forest and over the crumbling houses with a malevolent, linguistic sputtering that rang in the eardrum like the mechanical and crooked line of a stitch.

Earl Thomas had been in the room, watching her, listening to the buzzing insect: the sound rummaged throughout the house, the walls, and he wondered why had she sat there on the edge of the bed for so long a time when all it took was a motion of the fingers, a twitch of the limb, to abort the scene, the outburst she had created.

In conjunction with her precise and immobile composition, he had become erasable, drawn out by the error of an instrument—pencil lead—scribbled throughout the room without order. He was invisible.

Why not put it down? Move? he thought. And yet why hadn't *he* stepped forward, out of the agony of his standing place? He only stood there, as if sabotaged, trapped into statehood. He, too, had made the buzzing important, some conscientious observer to the party, the loud and terrible sputtering that clung to his position as if daring, saying to him that he longed to hear it. Even with his own life in jeopardy.

They. They. They. They were at once riveting, and he saw Curtis Willow, imagined it, his head trembling from the tumultuous blow, the face struck and turned aside on the ground. They had done it, driven him by wheelbarrow through town, so everyone could see, the head woven into a beast.

Emma New did not move: Earl Thomas stepped forward and disturbed the limb, the insect buzzing out of place and turn, before fleeing the house and out, out into the night air, the moon.

Emma New was out on the porch now. Her hair slept on her shoulders: she had abandoned the plaiting of it and reached out toward the wooden column, the wind taking part in her breathing.

Earl Thomas stood behind her a short while and returned to the room, closing the door behind him. He had whispered bleakly, Come in out of the dark; but the light of the lantern had accompanied her. He had no more faith in his own Word to make any of his announcements true.

He watched her from the window. A sudden absorption, an inward and solitary feeling, crept into a prophecy. He should not have stepped forward, disturbed the solemnity of the limb, when, at this moment, he wanted it, the systematic hurrying of the noise, the insect, the dream, the parallel line of the buzzing that she had composed—he thought, This must be what it's like. To be alone in the house. Alone without Emma New. Dead.

He wanted to go out onto the porch again, tell her, Come in out of the dark, come in out of the dark and let me . . . I don't know. Take you up? Hold you? But he couldn't. He had grown weary of thinking. Curtis Willow. Dead. Me. Dead.

His hand went up to the window and he wanted to include her in his gravity, his reaching out. But he could not draw her in. Emma New stood upon the world and was at the very base of the sphere, protruding out from her own axis, rotating in her gown, as if separation from him, the terrible thought of the dead, were the matters of her despondency.

He left the window.

And upon his absence, Emma New turned to face the cube from which he had looked out. Her hand surfaced the window, warm with the temperature of his breathing, and came down again: someone had crept up behind her, muzzled her mouth and throat.

She struggled, wanted to yell out to Earl Thomas, who had closed the door to the room and left her there. She reached for the lantern: the bitter light rose around her and the intruder and she spun, spun in his arms, until the glowing caught the flesh of his arm: she saw that he was pale.

Lord, she thought. They done come for 'm.

Suddenly, she stepped forward with her foot and brought it down upon the porch with a vernacular rumbling that shook the house.

Emma New?

Earl Thomas had come to a pause. He waited for it, a second rumbling.

Emma New had seemed so safe before.

Didn't come to hurt, whispered the intruder. Be still.

The words *Love him like he dead* were now unrecognizable to Emma New, as if Sonny had never spoken them. The encounter bashed the line, the memory, the agony of it, and she wished she had never believed it. But now, too late a time, she saw Earl Thomas—in her frightening and tumultuous predicament—spun by the web of insect and beast, spun by the white men, the spit of the tongue, flung from the house like poison and out into the wooded forest, the globe of his eye, the vein beaten out of familiarity, the skull.

Once again she lifted her foot and came down on the porch of the house.

She wanted to yell out to the world: Run, all o' you. Run.

A collective warning to the niggers, the jungle bloods, the men Earl Thomas's age and those to come. Run, all o' you. Run, they done come.

The door swung open.

Emma New had been swept from the window and away from the proximity of light. I ain't come to hurt, he whispered.

Earl Thomas stood before the intruder. A full-blown wind had leaped into him just now. He had practiced the coming of them, the theys, but had become so tired, so weak at this moment.

He and the intruder stared silently upon each other.

Emma New, yet bound by mouth and throat, reached out for Earl Thomas, and he no longer saw the woman who seemed so safe in the world. The lantern lit up her face, her fingertips, and held her in it, the beam underneath her gown, up toward the hips: the trembling.

Earl Thomas came out of his quiet.

Take me, he said.

The intruder let go of Emma New, who was sobbing uncontrollably. Her hair, wet with commotion, clung to her head. Her face sank low into the pitch of Earl Thomas's arm like a glossary.

Go inside, he whispered.

Emma New would not let go of him. Her face had not risen to light.

Go now, whispered Earl Thomas.

Emma New parted with him, until her sobbing disappeared into the fabric of the pillows.

The intruder lifted his empty hand from his pocket.

Sir, he whispered. Don't mean no harm.

Earl Thomas picked up the lantern and brought it up to the intruder's face.

What's your name, son?

Gill.

What you due for? asked Earl Thomas.

Gill stepped toward the eye of the lantern and spoke: I done wrong in the world. I done wrong . . . and I . . . I come . . . I come to help.

You come to hope? said Earl Thomas. How I know it?

I'm him, whispered Gill.

He said this with such agony, such electricity, that the rim of his eyelid fell downward and the thought of what he had done drew the creatures of the universe into a roaring collision.

Earl Thomas lowered the lantern: Come in, son, he said.

Gill Mender sat at the table of the Thomas house and emptied the contents of his pockets before Earl Thomas. Among them was the letter to Lenora Bullock. He simply wanted trust.

The lantern whistled between the two men: the flame rose, in a separate society, upward and down again, a streak of burning kerosene running up the belly of the transparent globe.

The light bound Gill toward it, and all of it, everything that he had done, spewed out of him. It leaked forward and away from his feverish body, and he told it and kept to his telling until his stomach was empty.

It had run through him so very quickly. His head began to swell, as though he were burning as the lantern was burning, as the moon above him burned in rotation and his chin lowered out of Earl Thomas's vision and he reached upward, over the globe of the lantern, his hand lit up and fascinating: he wanted to disappear, the blurred stench of a dirty gardenia.

Earl Thomas stood from his chair. He had heard the last of it. And Emma New had, too, heard it and was now sitting up from her pillow: a murmur eased from her lungs and into her throat, paralysis.

She lifted herself from the bed and slid her fingers beneath the mattress: the letter. Why did she want to give it to Gill now? Why was there a sense of far-reaching disclosure about her?

Her fingers drew upon the letters: *To the Men of the Pauer Plant. Courtesy of the Pastor.* She walked toward the lantern, the light, and placed it before Gill.

He spoke: I didn't mean to—

She interrupted: Take it.

Earl Thomas was too full to notice. He spoke: What's his name?

Nearly thirteen years ago the announcement had come that a boy had been born unto Hoover and D. D. Pickens, and now, as much as then, he knew that the pattern pointed to and looked at on the ground was his.

Gill stood, confused.

The boy come callin' for me, said Earl Thomas.

A silence throughout, and then he spoke: Adam.

The name and where it had come from, the first and beginning, the Father, punctured the silence of the room and bled into the stitch of Earl Thomas's rib and he held on to the edge of the table, the lantern wavering like a nude child.

His hand went up to his pounding heart, the chest within him, and he felt it growing tighter, the pounding, and wished it would go ahead, burst now, a river of blood around him, so they could grab hold of him and his bones, the wheelbarrow, take him up to Hurry Bullock's morgue and . . . He looked up at Emma New.

She was of no response, her little hand traveled up toward the back of her head, her face, and up to her hair. She had begun to plait the hairs of her head. A remote grin lifted her cheek. Adam, she repeated, and disappeared.

Gill walked toward Earl Thomas: Please, mister. Sit down. More coming.

Earl Thomas looked down at the contents Gill had emptied from his pocket and returned to his chair.

There fell upon him a repository of events that soon, he hoped, would bring the buzzing, the burgeoning memory of Curtis Willow, to a halt.

Sonny . . . Sonny, said Earl Thomas, a moan behind him. Tell it to 'er.

Gill responded, I run up on 'er there in the woods and I . . . I just couldn't, frozen.

Hurt, don't it?

Yes, sir, said Gill. It hurt and when I run up on 'er like that, I knew it was her and I seen 'er and she seen me and she . . .

Gill stood over the lantern and the flame, the rising wind of it, lifted a strand of his hair, and the heat burned the pupil of his eye— he tilted his face, his finger belted on his eyelid and the contents of the room, Earl Thomas, the chair grew blurry and out of range— he had stood too close.

You scared, mister? asked Gill.

Not now, said Earl Thomas. Not that the Lord done come.

Gill's hand abandoned his eyelid and he was without rhythm and ground there in the room. He had grown sicker than when he had come. The fever poured into him. With certainty, he was empty. Nothing left.

You good, son? asked Earl Thomas.

I gotta get home, mister.

Earl Thomas approached Gill: he was closer than he had ever been to another man, closer even than Curtis Willow, and his hand, in an effort to console him, rose from his hip and hovered over the blade of his shoulder.

But Gill interrupted, I don't deserve it.

And closed the door of the house. Gone.

Emma New entered the room, picked up a metal cylinder from a distant drawer, and smothered the oxygen of the lantern: He done come now, Earl. Time for bed.

Stung by the visit, the encounter, Earl Thomas staged himself perfectly. His feet were turned outward, an invisible peace woven throughout the darkness. And yet he deviated without familiarity into the clouded leakage of the lantern, reached forward to Emma New, gasped, and followed her to sleep.

chapter
twenty

A humming had taken place a short while ago. She forwarded the tune into expression, upright and away from the jawline. The piano. The music, it would come as she had hoped, and she would sit atop the wooden bench, her vertebrae adrift from her hip like the uncomfortable, sudden darting of snow.

The widow stood at the fabric counter. She reached into her pocket and retrieved a lavender coin purse. Her finger lay there awhile, near the embroidered pansy she had sewn into it. A singular, misplaced curve near the eye of the center drew her mouth into a perpendicular murmur. She wondered whatever had she been thinking to allow something so crooked to go so long a time in her pocket that it seemed to wage against the chiming of her own weight, bone.

The carpenter scanned her, wanted her to hurry. He had built a row of shelves behind the counter. The mailman was dead.

Ma'am, he urged. Ma'am, I best be going.

The widow's finger disappeared into the mouth of the lavender coin purse. She gave him a nickel. Here, she said. Come back tomorrow.

The carpenter opened his hand, the nickel had been dropped into it. There was a coldness about what she had done. What had she not today that she would have tomorrow? He looked upon her. He could have slapped her face.

But timidity had befallen him. He wanted to ask for more than this, more to get him home to Pyke County to feed his children—three of them waiting—but he gazed out, away from the sunlit window and into the mouth of the lavender coin purse. There was more there, more she could have given him.

Ma'am, he whispered. I've gotta get home. I've gotta get to—

I can't help it, she interrupted.

As much as he wanted to slap her face, *she* wanted to burst into compatible disgust. Upon his arrival, she had noticed the similar shape of his eye to that of her dead husband's, the commutable rotation of his shoulder: her husband would enter the house, hang up his coat—winter—and lay her out, her hair dirty and rotted with the stench of the Bullocks and Hoover Pickens, the morgue.

If it were never going to happen, if tomorrow, he were to come and she'd hold this against him, her fiendish and sickening posture, he may as well do it now, at this moment, when it seemed he had nothing more to hold on to.

The carpenter took his hand, large and uncompensated, and slapped her face.

She clung to his shock. Her face had not moved from its position. Indeed, she felt it, a ringing blow to the eardrum. She broke with laughter and paused a dangerous pause: Lopsided, she whispered.

He stared upon her, his hand yet trembling from the debris, the powder of her face. Never had he seen a woman, his wife included, hold such a violent temperature. His hand was still numb from it. His tools were at his feet; he reached down and took them up, the nickel in his pocket, and abandoned her.

The carpenter had offset her jawbone. Her hand toward her mouth, she realized what he had done. The taste of blood and saliva. Her lip had begun to bleed.

She walked away from the counter, past the piano—second-hand—and toward a box of tissues that lay on a lone shelf, a nail jutted out. Her mouth opened. The bloody saliva leaked out from the edge of her lip onto her dress. She was alone in the fabric store. No one had rung the bell.

A single blade of tissue, crushed by the discourse, the arrangement of her fingers, caught the bloody saliva. Her lip began to swell. And she took it, every bit of the swelling, and with her mouth yet open, she hummed from her throat.

But the bell *had* rung.

Lenora Bullock stood at the counter now. A pin trapped her yellow hair. The bracelet. The earrings. Costume jewelry from the morgue.

They belonged to the widow: Lenora had been at the morgue visiting Hurry when the widow's husband came through, a blow to the head: she reached over the corpse—a bulging envelope bearing the widow's name—and said to Hurry, Look, vanity.

Her face and wrist puckered, she turned to the mirror above the jungle blood and adorned herself with it. She whispered something, No blood on it. And looked down at her dress, emerald, and a surge of wind emerged from her stomach.

She was relieved: his upper torso, his face, had been covered by the sheet.

The bullet, she had seen neither where it entered nor came out. The widow, everyone knew she had done it.

She stepped away from the mirror ablaze, something new and hers, something belonging to the widow: Revenge, she thought.

For the widow had seen Lenora Bullock at the train station, waiting for a man from Bullock, had seen how she pulled the lip-stick out of her purse, put it up to her lips, and, out of malice, tapped her wrist, the red line going up the side of Lenora Bullock's cheek, smeared.

Was Lenora Bullock not, too, dirty?

The bell in the fabric store rang again.

Had she known the widow's first and born name, she still would not have called her to come. There was something in treating a person like he or she didn't belong. Her hand, suspended over the echo of the bell, came down again until the tune lingered and hung in the fabric.

The widow arrived at the counter, blood on her lip.

Anything good? asked Lenora Bullock.

The widow looked at Lenora Bullock: she was no more impor-tant in her exclamatory voice—the shiver of a broken bone—than anyone else in the world.

Well? said Lenora Bullock.

The widow reached for the lone item in Lenora and Hurry Bullock's mailbox: a Sears and Roebuck catalog.

It lay on the counter. Lenora Bullock took it up and flipped through the pages. Nothing in between. This was the only news.

Nothing from Vital Life? she asked.

The widow pointed to the row of boxes, a series of catalogs throughout.

We all got 'm, said the widow.

Lenora Bullock had just now paid attention to it, now that her letter had not come: the widow's lip had swelled outward, and without precaution, Lenora Bullock leaned over the counter and pointed to the swollen tissue.

That's what you get, she whispered.

The widow's face held the comment.

A noise plunged from the back room.

Lenora Bullock trembled, her hand forward: What's that yonder?

The widow, through the bulging lip, the tune, lied: My father.

Lenora Bullock, nothing from Vital Life, nothing with which to root her, stirred about and her hand clung to the yellow pin in her hair, the earrings, the bracelet, and she sputtered out of the fabric store like the irrevocable destitution of a carpenter.

Sonny had been standing beneath the limb of a tree when Lenora Bullock reached the center of the woods for home.

Lenora Bullock had come to a pause.

But Sonny, Sonny approached her. She stepped forward and into Lenora Bullock's breathing: she breathed her air and wind.

The costume jewelry. The blow to the head. The rigor mortis. There *was* blood on Lenora Bullock, and it rose above the two women, the calculation of a red blur in the eye. And the rotting of the blur, the leaking bondage and murder it had caused, spilled throughout the woods and deviated—a sort of vindictiveness—from its territory and down again into the discomfort of Lenora Bullock.

Sonny circled her there in the woods, around and around again, until Lenora Bullock's wrist went up to her mouth and the bracelet rummaged downward from her wrist and near the elbow. She was nude in her invisible speech. She had never been so close as now, close to the victim, the river of blood.

A bird flew above her and landed on a branch. For Lenora Bullock, in her perplexity, took it personally and inwardly: the bird had come to mock her, the vulnerability of her condition.

Sonny paused and looked ahead, beyond the pouch of Lenora Bullock's exhalation. She done took and took and took from all that was not and never hers and all that was never her husband's and the men, the men who took and took with him. None of it his and theirs, she thought.

Lenora Bullock, in her costume jewelry, released her hand from her mouth.

Sonny lifted her palm toward Lenora Bullock's lips, the startling complacency of her face, the murderous bones beneath drew her hand to a close.

Sonny had begun to howl and the bird left the branch and down, down toward Lenora Bullock: she had now broken out, a full-blown run, and the pin that trapped her yellow hair could not hold in her head. The howling . . . she was unsteady there on the ground and tumbled into the earth, her face and hair dirty, as dirty as it was when Hurry Bullock found her at the train station.

The encounter grew round in her head.

Lenora Bullock, in her tumbling, thought of Curtis Willow: he had come from the river—naked and alarming—the emaciated, hungry stream of the Mississippi dripped down the lead of his penis. His head turned with detachment away from her, his fingers near the thighbone with an inevitable spleen of embarrassment: the contours of his face and body singularly paused, his breath withheld.

A strict, staggering muscle pulsated in his face: his breath yet withheld, his eye wept and blended into the waters of the Mississippi.

He had simply gone for a swim.

With her bare hand, Lenora Bullock unbuttoned her blouse, the nipple erect and protruding, and touched him. The Mississippi dripped down her sternum, onto the flesh, and hung on the territory of her nipple.

Now she owned the interrogation, the full democracy of the muscular face, the penis: the birthmark, the thing she had claimed, resisted and pulled back, and she forced Curtis Willow's involuntary hand into her mouth and swallowed the river.

She released his hand. His arm swung from the shoulder and he could smell the powder of Caucasia—a catastrophic, infinite mutation that led him to pause.

Lenora Bullock yelled out: Nigger, you're dead.

Here, the silence, the paste of the nipple and breast, chilled him. She wanted to be.

He wished more for Lenora Bullock's freedom than she.

For the first time, he looked upon her. He lifted his hands to her blouse, gathered the fabric at the shoulder, and traced the socket of each button, bridging her self-esteem to a close.

She drifted with embarrassment, the rejection and exposure of what she had encountered, and ran through the woods, a fall ripping her skirt at the hemline.

She yelled out, screamed: A nigger, he whistled.

Now Sonny stood above her. Lenora took to her feet, the bird flying about, and ran until she reached her house and up the stairs: a cord of blood streamed from the remote and delicate bone of her ankle.

In her sobbing, the voice of D. D. Pickens seeped through: Leaves a stain.

She was so tired from the memory that she lay on the pillows of her bed and wished she were dead.

chapter
twenty-one

Hoover Pickens walked out of the barn and toward Midnight.

Come yonder, boy. He patted his hip, and Midnight's head went down into the dirt, his leg forward and back again.

Come, boy.

Midnight trotted in an adjacent and wide turn, away from Hoover Pickens. He halted in a gaze of inquiry. His head up now.

Adam stood behind the screen door of the breakfast porch: What you want with 'm, Papa?

Hoover Pickens froze in his beckoning, his face toward Adam. Salem's sick, he said. Midnight's gotta lay down with 'm.

What's he gotta do, Papa? asked Adam. Make 'm well?

Salem's coughing up blood, son.

Adam stepped onto the breakfast porch, the sun gone sour in the wind of his father's vocabulary.

Hoover Pickens squatted in the dust, his knee forward, and leveled his hand in the heat toward the gaze of Midnight. The sun had reached his shoulder and climbed upon the bed of his full arm. He was suffocating.

Midnight's gut shaped the ground, as if he had swallowed the killing at one time: of course, he had seen more than one killing—more than Curtis Willow—had lived long enough for the men to spill upon him their pitiful and horrid language. He had been called like this, asked to come here to this place, when D. D. Pickens knew, the world who made her, that he was not built to leak into their constitutions, their free-and-automatic-white-men speech; no one had tried, ever a time, to leave him be.

He barked at Hoover Pickens, his belly spewing out from the rib.

Son, said Hoover Pickens, go to 'm. Bring 'm yonder.

He had been asked to burn. His father was amid a rising flame, a sea of fire and heat: he had knelt into it there on the ground. It engulfed him and Adam could no longer see the head or the out-stretched arm, the foot. A burning, naked swimmer.

He won't come, Papa, he said. You see he won't come.

Son, responded Hoover Pickens. Call 'm to.

Adam stepped into the flame, the heat, and signaled Midnight toward him.

And he came.

Now, said Hoover Pickens. Take 'm up. Bring 'm yonder.

Midnight panted in Adam's arms, his head against the shoulder and bone he had saved at birth. Adam, in turn, looked down on him and gave him to his father.

Salem Bullock was sunken with sweat and fever. His entire body, his head, was wet and odorous, and the stench of his disparity flut-tered in the nakedness of his eye: the global rim of his pupil scanned the things of the room and he coughed, the vibratory context of the loud, auditory sound traveled through the sunlit window and into the league of morning locusts.

The bruised esophagus. The terrible, aching lung. His finger moved beneath the covers—the left side, congruent with the heart—he begged for mercy. Someone should have come by now.

The lung pounded within him. A figurehead, slanted and impetuous, hung in suspension over the lung. He thrust his hand forward and moaned. Nothing moved. He had no power.

He tossed beneath the figurehead, bound to the tail of it, a kite lifting him in the wind of hurry and detail, and he tossed and in his tossing, a button—weak from his churning—broke loose from his shirt. How he moaned, wanted to yell out to the fleeting of his moaning and to the kite above him to put him down.

He coughed from his lung, his finger confined to the gap of the missing button. And he began to stir with a remarkable, sudden urge to take to the kite and lend his weight to it and go up there, the clouds, the thirst of his rousing, and be new.

But there was no kite.

There was only a missing button trapped beneath the clavicle.

The tail of the figurehead slipped out of his moaning, let him go.

Salem, said Hurry Bullock. He done caught 'm.

He had come up the steps of the house, past the aligned photos of his and Salem's grandfathers, each to himself glorious in his formidable pose. The fingerprint of the widow's dead husband was yet pressed into the eye of Salem and Hurry Bullock's father: he had come to a halt at the bottom of the stairs, Him there? he asked. No, said Salem, pointing to the next father, the Wizard. Him.

Hurry Bullock shifted his foot in front of him. Nothing there, an invisible stain he pretended into view. He had shared the weight of his power with Salem, the two of them leaped into the dreams of their forefathers, two boys laughing and giggling in the heat and temperature of hedonism. It was unbearable to see him this way. He could only look down at his foot with inhibited dexterity.

Hurry, panted Salem Bullock. It's done low.

Hoover Pickens had arrived, stood with the two men, Midnight in his arms.

I bring 'm to lay down, said Hoover Pickens.

Salem Bullock was exposed now, his arms beside him in a straight line. The sudden pang of the button trapped beneath the bone of his clavicle caused his shoulder to rotate with discomfort. A moan crept, stirred.

It belonged to neither the Bullocks nor Hoover Pickens, but to Midnight. He had grown restless in the quiet of the room: he kicked, his head had succumbed to a particular inclination in the arms of Hoover Pickens. He wanted to get down, run.

Calm down, boy. Calm down.

Midnight sparred against him. He knew this scent, had been born into the pitch of the murderers' language and had swallowed it, all of the jungle bloods and niggers and the white men's hatred. And now he was to save him?

The aptitude of duty plunged into his eardrums.

Hoover Pickens forced him upon the covers of the bed: he squirmed with entrapment. He was a part of the stench, the sweat of Salem Bullock's rising lung, and he stumbled toward the organ and howled and barked at it, turned to face the two men who stood above him and down at Salem Bullock and then again at the space between the two standing men and struck out down the stairs and through the open door of the house.

Hurry Bullock followed him, a pistol on his hip, and fired . . . one, two, and the third shot knocked Midnight's leg out from under him . . . a piercing howl and nothing more. He was bleeding. Wherever he was, he was hit.

Hurry Bullock stood in wait: Goody for 'm.

The howling ascended up the stairs of the house, Hoover Pickens stood near the window. The firing of the gun, the third shot, the bullet and bone. Adam. The happening—quick and irretrievable—spun him into humility.

It's done low, whispered Salem Bullock.

Hoover Pickens abandoned him and traveled away from the house, past Hurry Bullock, the thing he had done crystallizing, and toward the trail of blood on the leaves.

Midnight would never come to Hoover Pickens, had never come.

Soon Hoover Pickens would look like, smell like, sour and obedient to the covers of his bed, Salem Bullock. He would beg for mercy, his hand over the throbbing organ that would turn him into a fine, rotted corpse.

When he approached the house, Adam met him.

Pa, what's the matter? Adam asked. The Lord done give Mister Salem some'n he can't handle?

Hoover Pickens knelt down before Adam, as he had to Midnight, and held his sobbing in the shadow of dirt below him. Son, he warned. It's Midnight. He's done shot.

The news, Adam stepped backward and away from his father. The sun danced in his hair and his weight, and his arms lifted from his thigh and in midair. Shock rose in his face, the mouth drained of reason.

Pa, Pa, shot, he's done shot, huh, Pa?

Hoover Pickens draped his arms around him, but Adam pushed back and away from the shirt and peered into the woods. Who done it to 'm?

He wouldn't lay down with Salem, said Hoover Pickens. He come out of it, pulled away. Hurry, Hurry took his pistol and fired a hit. Three o' 'em and Midnight went down somewheres.

D. D. Pickens ran out of the house: Hoover?

Adam collapsed in the dirt, heaved into the crux of his arm, and everything at once was dark and heavy and he couldn't breathe, the dust woven into his dilemma.

Hoover, repeated D. D. Pickens. What is it?

Hoover Pickens, perched beside Adam, answered her: Midnight's hit.

Adam abruptly rose from the dirt and ran through the woods until he caught wind of a trail of blood dotted upon the leaves. His head, bound to the dotted line, traced it and he ran up the hill . . . but the blood had run out.

Nothing there.

The following morning, D. D. Pickens discovered Midnight on the steps of the breakfast porch, his leg wrapped in gauze where the bullet had struck, pulled it out from under him.

chapter
twenty-two

Dog and men don't fit under the same covers: the doctor had come.

The sun poured down upon his hair. He towered about the porch and, for a moment, stepped away from Hoover and D. D. Pickens.

There, in the sentiments of the dust, lay a footprint. His—he looked at it, the sizable, narrowed arch of the setting, as if all he had ever been, now and coming, had lain there ahead of him, eclectic.

Seems they oughta: D. D. Pickens stood behind him. Her hand disappeared into the pocket of her gown, only her index finger jutted out.

The doctor stirred above the footprint. He lifted his face aside, his jawbone in a rude pause. The blur swam in his head, Hoover and D. D. Pickens: he had been here before, a boy, a dog, and entirely, the language of the people whose lives he had saved were each of the same bone and spirit . . . it was no matter, no one shaped the line to fit.

Midnight done used to one blood, ain't he, Doctor? Hoover Pickens patted his foot on the bottom step of the house.

Could be, said the doctor.

But not really had the doctor said this. Just now he wondered what he'd been thinking when the arch of his foot made the pattern, how come it had shifted so . . . and there was another one, another step forward in the dust, sideways like the morphological isolation of a moan.

You go on, he thought, mixin' dogs and men together. I'm done sick with it.

Doctor, said D. D. Pickens. He took to Adam. You seen how he took to 'm.

Her index finger had come out of the pocket of her gown and over her lips. The invisible, naked fumes reached her liver. The heat had simply drifted down her throat.

Although the doctor had not witnessed the happening, he stood in the circumference of Adam's revelation—under the weight of the doctor's thinking, Adam, bound by shock, had collapsed there beneath the footprint.

There in the dust lay the swirling remnant of Adam's bloated hand, the moribund, terrific round head where the news hung in the domesticity of the backbone.

The doctor looked down upon it: he saw now the less narrow of the two footprints, one unbelonging to him lying on the ground, nude and bare-boned. The other, a stage of momentary confinement.

I said you seen how it took to 'm, repeated D. D. Pickens.

The doctor's hand leaned in to his ribs. He wondered why at all she had not seen it. The stain. The tattoo. The boy had lain here and he was a part of the moan, the revelatory language of the news.

The doctor's lips parted.

He had swallowed a parlor of dust.

Now, he remembered how the postmaster woke him: he was wet with fever. A complaint about people, the world, drifted throughout the house. The postmaster gazed invisibly from the eye of the stethoscope and he asked him to breathe, breathe again, and in the pausing character of the instrument, what remained of people, the world was a tiny grove of oxygen uprooted from the postmaster's lungs, used and splattered, as if now that he wanted to live, the matter of his living was as dead and microscopic as the blow of its catastrophe.

The doctor had not saved. Not ever a time had he the breath and wind to lie down with the sick. He had only a mausoleum of footprints leading up to the houses, a stethoscope, gauze for a broken bone, and an inclination of which to test mortality. He was a ruse: it struck him inwardly and he seemed himself a part of the people, the world and language of the postmaster, the children he longed to save.

Hoover Pickens retrieved the elongated box the doctor had abandoned on the lopsided table and brought it forward. Doctor, he said. But the doctor was yet turned to him and D. D. Pickens, the sun left to weep in the false depiction of his standing. Here's your help.

The doctor could not bear it now. Doctor, your help. He had come to this house and the other houses and heard and listened, but they had missed it altogether: his own darkness had seeped through. He was pitifully cold.

He looked down at the footprint as if it reflected the debilitating coldness of his solitude, and, with his shoe, smeared it.

Show 'm, mercy, he uttered.

Hoover and D. D. Pickens stood as he had left them, a long howl from up high.

Midnight had begun to stir.

chapter
twenty-three

They rounded up their horses.

Pulled down their hoods.

Curtis Willow was a dead man.

It was dark out.

Gill was on the ground.

The men, his father, were on their horses.

Gill, said Hurry Bullock. Get up on your horse. You gotta do the talkin', son.

Gill took to Blade and the men began to yell and their yelling was all mixed up with hate and the hate was cold.

> We are white men, born unto the earth
> And land, which is ours and belongs to us, as
> Free and automatic white men.

They got down to the *burned before their properties* part: Hoover Pickens raised his pulley in the air. The line changed the pressure in his face.

Hurry Bullock kicked his horse in the side and yelled for Gill to pull out up front, all the other free and automatic white men following.

The moon shone through the trees. The thought of the dragging made Gill sick: he thought he'd come down off his horse and onto the ground. But Blade didn't notice that he was sick. The horse ran with him on it, the men behind him: the shouting stood in front of him in the darkness, ran in front of the horses, under the moon, through the trees, and guided the men toward the house.

Gill's shoulders sloped to one side. The running, panting horse led him through the woods. There it was: the house of Curtis Willow.

The horses, the men, came to a halt, a lantern in the window.

Hurry Bullock rode up beside him: Call out to 'm, son, he said.

His father drew his horse on the other side of him: Say it wheres he can hear it.

Go on, son, yelled the widow's husband.

Curtis Willow, said Gill. Come out yonder.

Hurry Bullock kicked his horse in the ribs and rode up to the porch: Curtis Willow! he yelled. Get out here, boy.

The curtain where the light had come from parted.

The door opened.

> *And whosoever shall fall on this stone*
> *shall be broken: but on whomsoever*
> *it shall fall, it will grind him to*
> *powder.*

Sonny stood on the edge of the porch.

You know what we come for, gal, said Hoover Pickens.

Sonny walked up to Hurry Bullock's horse: He comin', she whispered. His shoes . . . he's gotta get his shoes on first.

Hurry Bullock reared up on the horse, and the head of it struck Sonny's face. She fell on the boards of the house. She sat up and swallowed the blow.

A scream was caught in her face, but she would not do her screaming now.

Curtis Willow, yelled Hoover Pickens.

Curtis Willow had come out of the house: Heavy, ain't it? he moaned.

The widow's husband threw a bottle through the window, the house burning.

Sonny abandoned the porch, ran out near the maple tree.

Curtis Willow walked away from the porch and between the free and automatic white men.

And took it.

Hoover Pickens jumped down off his horse, Midnight barking.

The other men jumped down off their horses.

Curtis Willow disappeared between the sheets. They kicked him, and amid the kicking, his face traveled eastward, near the maple tree. No more Sonny.

Sonny turned away from the burning house and the hooded men and held herself, one hand on the tree, the other on her stomach, as if everything she had eaten up till now would explode and set the world, the moon, ablaze with hurt.

But she never made a sound.

Neither did Curtis Willow.

She let it go.

Curtis Willow's body curled up. The burning house lit up his shoes where he had shined them, so the moon, the world, could see the man he clung to.

They laughed collectively, shouted.

Curtis Willow—through the blood, the swollen head and face—looked up at the men, moaned: I'm already in your bones.

Nobody knew what the *heavy* was, if the hate was *heavy* or the world was *heavy* or the burning house. Whatever it was, he wasn't afraid.

Hoover Pickens tugged at the pulley.

The men roped him.

They jumped on their horses.

Gill kicked Blade in the ribs.

Hurry Bullock yelled out: We got us a nigger.

We got us a nigger, they repeated.

Blade pulled Curtis Willow and his body swung on the rope and his body turned in the blue light and he groaned and said, See how heavy it is? And the horse pulled him, his body churning on the ground.

Between the laughter, Curtis Willow's head hit a tree and the blood leaked from his face, wet on the earth. He groaned. His mouth had blood in it and he couldn't swallow the blood and hurt at the same time. He was a part of the moon and the trees: his body turned with the rope, and in an effort to lift his head from the ground, his neck grew tired and his head went down and the moon caught it: the bone snapped.

A bloody head.

Gill was sick, but the horse took him with it: he wanted to stop now.

He was so weak.

Not only had the bone head snapped, but the fingers, the ligaments.

Broken, torn apart.

The body hung, the feet in the pulley, until the hip gave way and made a sound through the trees.

Take 'm on through, yelled the free and automatic white men.

The horses led, took the body on through the forest.

There was mud on his shoe.

The free and automatic white men laughed: We *know* it now, said Hurry Bullock.

The nigger's dead.

The nightmare flung Gill out of it.

The burning house, *the nigger's dead,* the swollen head swam a line throughout his hair, sooty. He emerged from the bed—the body had lain there, full and alive in its dreaming—he was still breathing, a sudden gratuity.

In rotation, the sound of his mother's whispering beneath the covers, his waking, spun him around collectively: he pointed toward the window and down at his foot. The circumference of his standing pushed him forward, as if a drowning had taken place of which he had been a witness and could only now part his lips.

The single step forward, the sudden immobility of how far and little he had reached, struck his rib like the iron pedal of a piano. The tune swirled around him and down his throat and he began to manipulate the echo of the thing he'd heard, his hand traveled downward to the strict pattern of his shirt. He had offset the tune, the isolated rhythm of the winding murmur.

With his being dead, it was no wonder he saw the men come for him, the wheelbarrow sounding throughout the woods. This was the tune he'd heard. The men had come for him. He lay corpsed and frozen with rigor mortis and they stood, each in his own number, and picked him up by the shoulder, put him in the wheelbarrow.

The sun had come down upon him, his face and head swollen, and they laughed around him, a gurgling sound to imitate the final blow of the world. They had come for the tiny bird in the woods, whoever could have heard it to begin with, when it was born as if never to be heard by anyone at all? They paused for a moment, looked at the anatomy of the eye, how it'd come out so *good* from the head, and one of them, a blur, reached into the wheelbarrow and squinted. Ripe, he said.

And plucked it.

The illusion Gill had succumbed to, the men surrounding him with laughter, sent him scavenging about the room. He was not a nigger. Not in the wheelbarrow. Not apart of the laughter of men. He was one of the men. It was he who said it, Ripe.

The echo dispersed: Curtis Willow. Come out yonder.

The moon led him away from the house. He paused, balanced his foot on the ground, the tune in his head. When the gurgling found him—the sound of it pitiful—he ran from the house and upon the earth and through the trees until he reached Sonny Willow: through the open window, he saw her.

She was naked.

Curtis? she asked.

She turned to the window, Gill Mender exposed.

The pulse of the moon shone on his throat and he backed away, away from the window, the thing he had come to do.

But he had not at all moved.

Sonny Willow's arm had risen from the window and trapped him at the shoulder: Been wait'n.

The tune had come to a halt.

Sonny Willow, now in her gown, opened the door of the house. A lantern had been lit in the room, the belly of the globe drew them inward, one to another. The expansion of silence—the breathing of the two bodies—clung with the pale diversion of vertebrae.

Sonny Willow could have touched him: he had run in her dreams, barefoot and white—the dead odor of a gardenia—and turned with laughter, his tiny hand lifted above his head.

The enemy, the bones she had pictured, shook within her slumber, a hum that slept behind her eye, and the boy, she could never catch him, eluded her and left her near the foot of the maple tree.

She remembered the crescendo of the voices: they had come from the esophagus, the battered murmur of the lung.

Her hand rose above the globe of the lantern: her finger on the base of Gill's throat, she calculated the length of the bone, the age and species of the seasons, and retrieved her hand into the bosom of the wet gown.

What he look like? she asked.

Bloody.

Tell it to me like it done to 'm, she said.

They: when he said *they,* Sonny Willow's hand pointed toward *him* and he arranged the duty of the line to fit his responsibility. We—after we called 'm out, we took 'm through the trees and the pulley . . . some'n caught 'm and Hurry Bullock said to keep running. So we . . . we brought 'm to the end of the line. His eye come out.

Sonny Willow paused.

Gill's telling of the murder, what they'd done to Curtis, exposed his vulnerability. Without pity, she could take the lantern, come down upon his telling of it and set him ablaze. *His eye come out* drew her bones forward, and for the first time, she could not refer to Curtis in her head. She had forgotten, just now, the definitive detail of the pupil upon waking, the shape of the globe in his face.

His eye come out. The announcement struck her: when Curtis walked through the trees in the morning time, she never turned in her standing, only envisioned the face, the symmetry of the bones, and now, the news of the happening tilted her head aside, as if she yet stood at the foot of the maple.

She signaled for Gill to quiet.

In her solitude, the naked vocabulary of her thinking, she asked: Why not take me? Her hands drawn together, she winced upward, away from the globe of the lantern in the comparison of a man befallen to a blade.

Gill stood from his chair.

Ma'am, ma'am, did they bring 'm to you?

Her hand opened, a stir of unbound reciprocity. Hurry Bullock had done it to her Curtis and soon, soon to Earl Thomas.

They would ground him into powder.

And now, the *Hurry* and *Bullock* Curtis had spelled upon the palm of her hand evoked within her a constellation, a discovery of her own anthropology.

It was hers, belonged to her, and no one—man nor beast—could claim it.

They brought the bones, she whispered.

Where'd you put 'em? asked Gill.

Her eye lit in the stirring of the globe: The maple.

In the morning, she would bind a cross together, a single nail to confine the wood, now that she knew the entire happening, the recantation of the whispering bones, the blood.

chapter
twenty-four

The widow's hair—bound by a ribbon—had come loose this evening.

The upper torso, her shoulders, in the face of the mirror.

She had begun to hum.

The fabric of the ribbon hung from her fingers. No one was here now. No one had rung the bell. She looked upon the ribbon and, in her carelessness, dropped it on the floor.

The humming, the interruption of quiet, drew upon the things of the room. A note she could not remember paused in her head: she looked at the ribbon with uncommon decency, a peculiar nerve trapped in her eye.

She vanished altogether from the mirror and started from the beginning of the line, but it would not hold. Her hand went up to her head: she had returned to the suffocating line only to forget, again, the continuation of her humming.

A pulsating vein rose from the crux of her blouse, upward into the settling jugular. It had run so quickly—immediate and rushing—into her position. No one had mocked her. No one heard the corpse of the tune. But she stood this way, as if everyone had heard it and mocked her: a carpenter had walked into the room, slapped her face, and she took it, but this, this she could not take.

She swung her head around—the line would not come out—and the odor of what she had succumbed to sifted throughout her dirty hair and down her eardrum. The mocking, she could not stand it. She yelled out, screamed.

But no one was in the world.

She was alone in the fabric store.

And she was as dirty as she had been when she entered the train station.

She hurried toward the piano and began to play. The keys panged in the echo of the room and the note . . . what was it? What key? She could not recall the flame of the key, as she could not the note, but she played on. It *would* come.

It would come soon.

If ever God was abundant in her thinking, it was now, at the piano. Perhaps, if she sang it aloud, the key would strike the cord and she'd fix it the way things ought to be fixed, the way sick men lie in their beds—a pistol to the back of the head.

Down below her, the ribbon lay as she had dropped it: her wrists shifted from the keys. She made a fist, one hand in the air, and came down on the piano, cursing the tune with a whisper.

It was no wonder she had not heard the bell.

It rang again upon the lighted piano, the keys yet trembling with urgency.

D. D. Pickens had been standing there all the while: she had peered behind the counter and seen the untamed hair of the widow, the wrists bellowing out from the piano.

In her queer predicament, she interrupted: Anybody there?

Someone was there and she well knew it.

The widow had not responded. Her hand rose toward the jugular and she pressed down on the vein, as if to quiet the restlessness of her sudden, ecliptic transition.

D. D. Pickens was inconsistent. Of course she had woken from her dreaming, stood at the cracked fissure of her window, and recalled to memory the question from her own Hoover Pickens: *What do you want?*

This evening she had neither pondered nor weighed the naïveté of her response. She had solely asked him to *Look at it.*

Now only the lighted star remained.

The wind of the piano placed a tremor upon the widow. She stood at the counter, her arms at her waist in some vibratory momentum. She grew uncomfortable in the blouse and patted her throat near the neckline.

It had come to her why the tune had vanished this evening: her name was embroidered into a lone patch of yellow fabric that clung to her collar by the arm of a straight pin. The silent note struck her face, and with her index finger, she tugged the pin loose, the yellow patch on the counter.

And so it was written: *Quill.*

D. D. Pickens spoke: I come for the news.

The widow turned to the mailboxes. Pickens, she murmured.

She returned to the counter with two envelopes and laid them before D. D. Pickens as if she had never come here. She opened a cigar box adjacent to the two envelopes and stuck her finger in it.

D. D. Pickens came to a halt: a spider had begun to crawl on the bed of the widow's fingertip and up toward the elbow.

The widow's head leaned aside. Her hair sloped outward from the bone of her shoulder and hung in the wing of her serenity. She disappeared from the counter and drew the fabric up to her hip.

The spider trampled upward as her hair fell upon the keys of the piano. She had risen from the crowded laughter of her dementia.

Her foot reached the pedal. The tune had come out of her humming now, the forgotten and indelible line of the season sprung forth into her memory.

Suddenly, the nail above the piano seemed so sturdy in D. D. Pickens's mind, pleading it was: she forced her eye into it, the blunt head of the instrument leaking through the pupil, a fine red line of blood traveling through the lobe and down toward her gut, like dye, and into the pouch of her vagina. It had come out in her mind and she spread her legs apart, as if she waited for it to drip onto the blur of the wooden floor beneath her.

The tune of the widow shook her, the mockingbird bone hollering out for attention, and she was, at once, near the window, dripping and wet, Hoover Pickens behind her, his penis pushing the fine red line up again into her vagina, and had asked, and the asking plunged into her memory: What do you want?

Grace had given her something she didn't deserve. It sat up in her stomach, a stone. The tune of the widow mocked her and her arms went up to her eye, her stomach, as if she expected the weight of a bird to come out in the fine red line: she stood by a maple and a wind would come, push her down, and she would have to . . . take to her death.

The tune had come to a pause.

The spider disappeared beneath the collar of the widow's blouse and up toward the cranium. She began to laugh and quiver in the blouse, her head forward upon the keys. Her hair trembled wildly and she looked at D. D. Pickens—her legs yet apart—and commenced to playing again, the spider weaving a hole in her skull.

chapter
twenty-five

Hoover Pickens had never seen it as now.

Adam walked Blade up to the breakfast porch: he was fully dressed in the Klan suit and hood, his hands on the reins of the horse, as he dictated the arch of the ribbed muscle, a full step forward, the hooves kicking up the dust behind him.

Another step backward, a pause.

Blade breathed through the full nostril of the commandment: his belly hung low from the saddle, Adam's foot on the lung of his breathing.

Hoover Pickens stood on the breakfast porch: the contours of the wide-brimmed hat lived in his hand, the sunlit beam of the earth traveled down the surface of his wrist and onto the buffalo hide.

Not since Adam's fall from Hurry's training horse had he seen this. He opened his mouth and let the sun in it: he was so clean right now—a clean man—and when he'd let the sun in, he swallowed the heat and the roaring of the hooves on the earth.

He dropped the wide-brimmed hat and walked toward Blade. The night of Curtis Willow's death had befallen him, and he saw in his full eye the nigger step down from the porch and, too, Sonny holding her gut near the maple.

The crowing of the wheelbarrow, the corpse—how they had beaten him, the bloated kidney, the organs pushing the belly out— and now, now that Blade had come again to rouse the slumber, the *heavy* sleep, he could not contain it. His arm went up to his face, up to the eye, and he turned from the horse and Adam, as if by turning he could remember it fully.

He paused, a grin.

Nearly thirteen years ago now, the pastor had come to show him something, early morning, and he had slapped his face. The nerve of that nigger to reach out to him.

Earl Thomas was dead.

And he well knew it.

A vertical line struck the center of his face, a vein: he should have done it long ago. So close. Had anyone in the world known how patient he was—to hold such a thing, an encounter—in his head and body for so long a time that it seemed now all the more reason to kill?

It was no wonder the kite had come down.

To take . . . to disturb the free . . . it was owed to him. For he had no fathers or grandfathers aligning the flight of stairs in his house. He was the beginning.

The father.

A threaded seam of evaporation was woven into Hoover Pickens. It hummed in the womb—a piano—and upon his birth, the music, the tune descended from the bone and into the sterile wind of a cloud.

A pang shook him: he held his ribs.

Son, you done it, he said, his free hand on the belly of the horse. He's done new.

Adam kicked Blade in the ribs: the horse trotted around his father. The course of the pattern vibrated in the dust.

Adam kept it within, the interrogation of the man who disturbed the axis of his vocabulary: You let Mr. Hurry shoot 'm, he thought. Look what he done.

He pulled the reins of the horse and paused.

His father was a part of the dust now. He had knelt down, his hand up to his belly, the other on the earth. The sudden pause of the trotting held him diametrically inward, the scope of the 360-degree pattern seeping throughout the heated and porous sweat of his position.

Blade emerged from the pause and again encircled him.

An extraordinary moan dispersed from Adam's lips. The two holes cut into the Klan hood, the synonymous gaze of the eye, reflected a term of embarrassment.

Not for his father but for the thing he had become. His father had always been this, this coward in the dust, he who could not hold a pang in his stomach while standing, as he could not hold it lying down.

Hoover Pickens was a foreigner.

It was the scent of Midnight that Adam remembered.

He had come to tears beneath the hooded Klan suit.

Adam had overheard his mother tell it to Lenora Bullock: the morning of his conception, his father had pushed her tangled hair from behind and into the sunlit window, and when he pulled out, a whisper, the semen blurting, an explosive, unbearable plea from the vagina, unheard and battered.

Lenora Bullock, in the polarity of her language, grinned and responded, looking down at the pie she'd brought that evening: all the time it took.

Adam was a part of the vagina, the cracked fissure of the window, the woman who had traveled through the clouded wood and brought Midnight to save him.

Hoover Pickens's head plummeted forth. The distance of the earth and sun crept into his kneeling as the dust spun around him: he lay there on the verge of metamorphosis. He could not, at will, digest the pang in his stomach with the good, the trotting of the horse and Adam. A private instability, a moan of bewilderment, trembled in the tomb of his lung and he turned on his side, the silhouette of a throbbing uterus.

Midnight's head shone through Adam's open window. He lifted his chin above the horizontal plane of the sill. A pink cloud drifted into the obscurity of his pupil. The blood clot caused by the bullet was dispersing.

Adam looked down at his father:

> *And whosoever shall fall on this stone*
> *It shall grind him to powder.*

Adam gathered the reins collectively and struck the ribbed muscle.

Blade sparred in the dust.

Ya! yelled Adam. Ya. Ya. Ya.

And thus altogether disappeared.

chapter
twenty-six

It was nighttime.

A dew of perplexity drifted among the free and automatic white men: they had positioned the wheelbarrow—its head askew—in the wooded forest, until the creatures of the earth grew irritable, sick of their laughter, and hummed to one note, one striking crescendo, and ran them out of it.

Now the free and automatic white men stood in the mouth of Hoover Pickens's barn.

The moon had encroached upon them the insoluble mannerism of agony.

Hurry Bullock was polluted: a bottle of whiskey lay beneath his shoe. He had begun to weave from his standing place, his head downward and a part of something, something pitiful.

Gill Mender and Hoover Pickens spoke around him, and the voices—the two men at once—spurted in the blood of the moon. They were a collective blur.

The bottle of whiskey rolled out from under Hurry's shoe. He motioned with his index finger a plea: Come here.

He turned to face the collective blur and pointed at the ground that held him. But the men clung to their laughter and pointed at *him*. The voices swiveled with profound digestion. His hand out, forward: he wanted to say, Salem, Salem's dead.

But the moon caught it. The whiskey laid the tongue down.

A murmur.

He breathed inwardly, and his head and face struck the wind of illusion: he groveled, stepped forward into the blur, as if to grab hold. Salem, Salem's dead, he whispered.

But no one heard.

He seemed to the men around him to stand in one place, one hand reaching out in the depiction of a dirty gardenia. Go home, Hurry, said Hoover Pickens. Go home.

Look at 'm. Weak.

The word panted and dove into the face of Hurry Bullock. His mouth fitted the symptoms of a stroke: the divided line faltered, a perpendicular beam of saliva spilled out.

He lifted his finger in the direction of the blur and weaved forward: Salem, he whispered . . . Salem's dead.

His head lowered, he turned to the empty ground and exploded with laughter. He ran his finger down the bone of his hip and came up again, as if he had been drowning the whole time.

The laughter shattered his lung. He peered down at the earth—something said of sleep, a man upon waking—his hand lay flat on his belly. The temperature and pulse of a moan wept in the organ.

He wandered through the mouth of the barn: he swallowed, patted the hem of his larynx. Suddenly, he took part of the moon blood, his vertebrae erect.

When a man is drunk, a precise and particular image carves upon him the magnetism of his ill-belonging to anything else in the world. Hurry Bullock—the whistling sound—the bottle of whiskey had been pushed farther into the dust; he sent it sputtering

with announcement and circled the air with his fingertip, winding it down, winding the tune of the echo down until at once his
thumb and index finger drew a unanimous bridge—both together
silently, a stroke of telepathy.

The image stood before him: Adam.

Adam *was* the precision—the thing he could not blur—and he
grew closer, closer toward him, and he knew that it was Adam.
They were conjoined, the moon blood took the bone, the face of
the shadow.

Hurry Bullock: I done come to, he said.

When he said *I done come to,* he meant, of course, that now,
now the world had let him in it and he could see the image, no
longer a mirage of weak and insidious laughter, clearly in the full
skirt of his eye: he stood as if pleading for Adam to take part in
the responsibility that he had just then . . . possessed.

His vertebrae had come out of alignment with his hipbone.

And then, the shot fired, his finger on the trigger and the howling rung in his eardrums, he pulled back and the howling of Midnight ricocheted in the moaning lung.

Hoover Pickens was in the barn showing Gill Mender the archival packages retrieved from the corpse of the wheelbarrow.
There it was: the brown envelope.

For Sonny.

Hoover Pickens mocked: For Sonny. For Sonny. He had become
a replica of the memory, the free and automatic white men who aped,
as he, the mannerism—the striking bone of the Neanderthal—the
dead nigger.

The vulnerability of his lying in the dust had not occurred to
him: Hoover Pickens had crushed the footprint of the doctor—of
Adam—in the dust with archaeological distortion, a willingness
to forget.

Isn't this proof that I've lived long enough to hold it? He set the brown envelope to the light of the lantern and then toward Gill, as if to say: *Look what I've done.*

Gill partook of the scene. He rotated the blade of his shoulder with an expression of repulsion: the navigable vein of Hoover Pickens's jugular pulsated under the lantern. Gill's finger slid down into his pocket—a box cutter from the train station—he could slit his throat.

But yet he stood and held the brown envelope: For Sonny, he mocked, and Hoover Pickens stirred with laughter, the jugular protruding outward in the season of the once-muted room: he held his stomach, his hand ahead of him and up to his head, primitive.

He appeared suspended, hung by the esophagus, the muscle of his forearm spiraling under the shirt, near the elbow. The energy of the room held him in it, and awkwardly, he thought of Adam, the horse, as if this were the bait of his suspension.

You done it, he yelled. Oughta seen 'm. Downright proud.

Gill was no longer in the archival room, but stood clean of the lantern and watched as Adam, doused in moon blood, walked up to Hurry Bullock and spat in his face.

chapter
twenty-seven

The cold nipple stood erect from her gown.

Lenora Bullock's face turned toward the window, her arm above her head, as if she could not decipher, even in her dreams, the throbbing birthmark from the perishable resistance of her own temperature: the moon stood in the room, silently chirping above the house, as if it knew the calamity of her breathing.

Hurry Bullock was cold tonight: he lay there beside the missis, her nipple frozen.

The loose hair of her head hung down over her shoulder where she had trained it to suit her slumber, hung there and rose as she breathed on the breast of her pale body: he could have taken her now, as she slept, woken her from the category of her quiet position.

But no, he would not wake her. He would lie there, listen to the breathing of this creature, as she lay there with him—of all the *hims* in the world—and was.

By some uncertain cause, there is a moment when a man turns to the sleeping wife beside him and is so offset by her sleeping that he cannot maintain the matter of his thinking, when it seems she is only a measuring rod of which to adjust his failure.

And yet it was she who had adjusted.

He could wake her now, if he wanted.

She was so vulnerable, so destructible: it was her face, the indescribable one that seemed so perfect in its caged bone—there was no moving muscle, no sound coming out.

Thus, he wanted to wake her, wanted her to say *What is it?* So he could emit some sort of power, tuck her language down, down into the caged bone.

Hurry Bullock was alone in the world.

He could not sleep so peacefully as she.

His finger drifted toward the nipple: he pinched it.

But she did not say *What is it?*

She only whispered, Hurry?

Two people—lying down together—indeed, whisper one to another and yet inwardly into the gut of a rising cloud: the vertical position of slumber, the him and her, stirs with transparency the naked and battered eardrum.

When she said this, *Hurry?*, she now seemed to him eponymous.

The scent of the train station—she was dirty when he found her, dirty, and the debris of her bastardism was thrown about her face and hair.

It was no wonder he pulled out: dirty women bleed into their babies. The thought carried, shifted throughout, and he could only imagine a Bullock floating in the debris of the embryonic fluid, the face molded and corruptible like the jagged edge of a blur.

She again whispered, Hurry?

He turned, without response, away from the cold nipple, the indestructible breathing, and wished, if ever a time, that he, too, were dead.

chapter
twenty-eight

Now, you, too, must.

Earl Thomas could not think of dying now, when he knew how alive he was.

Night had come: his face darted in the moonlit wood—the shadow of the news he bore shattered the bone of earth beneath him.

Now he had come to the wheelbarrow, propped there in the woods by Hoover Pickens or Hurry Bullock or one of the other free and automatic white men, and remembered the bloody head, the nailing shut of the upper and lower mandible, the eye.

Of the things he'd heard, the swollen torso was what shook him.

The buzzing rigor mortis: the battered bird had been dragged here, the shoe slipping out from his foot, and he could hear it, the buzzing maggot of the corpse, the final moan parting, with conclusion, into the mouth of the Mississippi.

The moon struck the wheelbarrow and Earl Thomas equally. How innocent it looked, the thing that carried the dead, as if weeping from its own metallic throat the announcement of the weighted blows it had brought to and forth stained upon its character the aura of solitude.

Earl Thomas, the moon burning, lifted the index finger of his free hand and touched the singular parallel bar of the handle. His head forward with intimacy, there seemed to live within him a disturbing rattle of echoes, altogether and unified, one sound and one blood, the discriminatory yelling of the murderer: Nigger, you're dead.

He let go of the parallel bar and drew his fist together and upward into the living sound of the crowd—like electrification—and pushed through it and was pounded upon, pounded about the face and head and the conclusive and weighted blow of the vertebrae that at once paralyzed him, his arms, legs, numb in the bladder of voices around him.

Earl Thomas, you're a dead nigger, said the voices. And you know it.

He wanted now to turn back, back to Emma New, and await the yelling of the crowd, but the thing he had been sent to do hung over him—sharp and viscerally—that he must, for Emma New, for Sonny, take part of the blade, the perforated stench that had come and returned men like him swollen and lung-pregnant to the earth.

Of course, he knew that it was neither earth nor wheelbarrow to blame.

He held on to the envelope and again ran through the eye of the forest, until at last he reached the house. A slow breath parted in the wind.

He was a man, had always been.

Now he was in it. He held on to the envelope and saw the first step, the open door, the pale fabric of the bitter gown that hung in the house: the woman—her face up to the window—paused in her locality. A crooked line bled through the center of her scalp. Her hair, uncombed and dirty, was without poise and sat on the bed of her shoulders amuck.

She had not whispered *Hurry?* by reason of her nipple being pinched.

She had fallen out of a dream, spilled forward beneath the sheets, a self-inflicted wound of which she had meant to call to and forth the face of the term: *Father?*

She spoke: That you, Hurry?

Now she stood in the door and saw, with shock, the depth of her questioning: she had rehearsed it subconsciously . . . if a nigger ever come close to her, she would . . . she would do something wonderful, take a knife and . . . she could not remember.

A bitter paragraph of confusion shaped itself around her.

And yet she was unafraid.

I . . . I . . . said Earl Thomas, the envelope in his hands. I come to help.

The wonderful thing she would do somehow stood in the distance, but then she hunted it down in her head—something else— and opened the screen door of the house, wiped her hands on her gown, and slapped his face.

She trembled with exhaustion, the shock and bold nature of his coming there so close with no one left in the house but her and her alone.

He began to speak.

She spat in his mouth.

He swallowed it.

Her own cruelty caused him to forgive, when she appeared so hopeless, pitiful, never knowing. He lived within her all the while.

An atmosphere of fragility soared above the burning of his face.

He looked down at the envelope and opened it, whispered.

Why do you search for me? read the letter. *I am already in your bones.*

When Lenora Bullock heard this, a fever shook her, the terrifying line in her head, the thought of being a a a . . .

In her delirium, her mouth parted, as if she had been lying in the morgue—dead and frozen—the paternal whisper of the jungle blood and bone wove a beast around her: Ape, it said. Ape.

Earl Thomas had reached the wood, disappeared.

The letter was at her feet: she knelt down beside it, this thing that held and spun her out of normalcy, and turned to the letterhead, Vital Life Office.

It was then that she fainted on the porch of the house.

The dust went up her nose, staining the flesh of her birthmark. She lay there for a time, the hairs of her head jostled about, until the dust grew unbearable.

She began to cough.

When she fully came to, she opened the door of the house.

There, on the mantel, lay the pistol, as Hurry had left it.

With urgency, she ran toward the barn, climbed the ladder up to the second tier, the third, and leaned her head in to the pistol—the nose hidden beneath the earlobe—she grinned and then . . . then the sound of the bullet shook her head, causing it to turn as she fell from her place.

The ground caught her.

She broke a rib, the bone shook her gown.

The pistol had fallen out of her hand: a little bit of her brain oozed out onto the shoulder, blood spewing forth from the edge of her jawbone.

Hurry Bullock had come from the morgue.

He heard the shot and ran up the stairs of the house, no Lenora, and down again to the silent window that had not long ago held the warm matter of her face.

The empty house, the silence of things unbreathing and motionless, settled in his stomach: he paused near the table and looked down beneath him—a thread had come loose from her gown and pointed eastward.

It lay upon the palm of his hand.

Only he stood in the room and only he had done it.

With uncertainty, he faced the mantel: the pistol. Gone.

The thread, loose from her gown, floated amid the revelation.

Hurry Bullock had begun to weep: he opened the door and revisited the steps, the rushing out of Lenora, and found her lying, the brain oozing out behind the earlobe, the forehead, and turned her over with his full hand.

Now that he could no longer touch her, he—himself—seemed extraordinary, the dotted scope of a figurehead.

He walked backward, away from the gown, the gunpowdered stain of the pistol, and hollered. But the hollering had come to a halt.

Someone had crept up behind him, knocked him unconscious.

And, too, the night woke like a running, ill-fated beast, and Gill woke with it, leading Hurry Bullock's horse through the forest's opening until the Pickens's house burned in his head.

The moon, with its round and full belly, shone acutely—a blunt stroke of light darting out—and gazed upon his entire purpose an exaggerated beam; it struck the anatomy of his face, pointing downward with its fingertip an abbreviated, piercing moan.

Gill had come to a stop, looked up, up to the window where Adam was, and seen him peering down on him.

The stench of Lenora Bullock lay in the fabric of Gill's clothing: the oozing out of her brain on her shoulder, the bullet cascading through her birthmark.

Hoover Pickens stood in the mirror of his bedroom: he stepped backward, away from the shifting disease of his body, as if by doing this, he could adjust, abandon the sickness, give it away to reflection.

But he could not.

His finger rose in midair, following a hallucination, a dotted line woven by the shattered lung, the fever. All this time he had been laughing singularly.

No one had ever joined him. Not when it was his own body and spirit that had done and lived with such violence that it swelled in his esophagus and moaned when he moaned in the morning time.

He had lived a duration of many years within a destructible village, a calling out of the breath to distort, disfigure, the things of the world and the God they belonged to.

There would be no sunlight in this room now, nothing to strike the wrist, no other creature to join him in the perpendicular beam of the house. It was nighttime. And the moon had grown tired of his kind.

He paused, D. D. Pickens looked upon him with a surrogacy. Whatever was it that had brought them together? What thing had they been strung upon, separate and unapproachable in the room?

Or perhaps, in her stance, she knew more than ever that she had always been, that they, together, had always been dirty and without, without anyone or anything to draw them closer in this room or another, this one or the pitiful orphanage of a train station.

She lifted her hair from her shoulder in his presence, walked toward the window where the cracked fissure lay parallel to the whisper she had committed herself to, and turned with her nude and exasperated body: What do you want? she asked.

Hoover Pickens, as he had been so tired tonight, stepped forward and back again, away from her and the cracked fissure, as if
now that he had been faced with his own questioning, he could
not bear it, did not want it living in his mind: he stepped forward
again, peeled the sheet from the bed, and clothed her with it, but
she did not hold on, she let go of it and he turned aside, his face
anew, and altogether gazed upon a distant, conclusive matter that
belonged to him and solely him.

Weak? she asked.

But then he heard the horses, Blade and the others let go from
the barn, and pushed her aside, looking down below . . . Blade was
saddled, Adam roaming around in the dust aboard him, kicking
up the moon glow, the dust baiting upward, away from the . . . he
ran down the stairs, out of the house, and amid the running horses,
his hands beckoning to Gill: What's done it?

The horses rippled around him, Gill pulled on his reins, signaling to Adam: Lenora. She's dead.

Hoover Pickens paused, closer to Gill: Dead?

Gill nodded.

Everything spun so quickly about, the words, Lenora. She's dead.
That Hoover Pickens kneeled to the ground, his hand balancing
the root of the announcement.

Then, then what . . . then, he stumbled through it and wanted
to ask where Hurry was and who done it, but his wind left him.

Adam stood next to Blade now.

Gill jumped down, let go of his horse, and handed Hoover
Pickens the letter: that nigger, Earl Thomas . . . he's who done it.

Hoover Pickens took the letter and stepped toward the lantern
on the breakfast porch, D.D. in her gown near the window. He
saw the heading, Vital Life Office, and read the opening space of
the line: *Why do you search for me? I am already in your bones.*

With this, he thought of Curtis Willow, the night of the drag-ging and how arrogantly the nigger spoke, aloud and between the blows of him and the other free and automatic white men, and the letter drifted from his trembling hand, and thus the rage of his brow landed evenly with the wilted expression of his lips, and at once he ran up the stairs of the house, braced himself in his Klan suit and hood: another thought plagued him—the morning he pinned Earl Thomas down at the Pauer Plant—he stood before the mirror, recited the constitution of the free and automatic white men, Some nerve, he whispered, and struck it.

He ran down the stairs of the house, D.D. near the window in a phase of bewilderment: Lenora's dead.

The news crept upon her and the dirty line she'd forced upon Lenora Bullock—*leaves a stain*—lifted her hand to the table and she breathed inwardly, took and inhaled the item of her thinking: it was the momentary agent, both she and Lenora, their faces smudged and baited at the train station, waiting for a man from Bullock to resuscitate, restore, that flung her out of context.

A spider crawled near the windowsill and its tune struck her with infection, a whirling tune she had made up like that of the widow, the piano, and whirled around and within her throat, as she lifted her fingertip in front of her. The spider trampled upon the bed of her arm, beneath the blouse, and near her larynx: she opened her mouth and ate it, the blood rushing through.

Hoover Pickens walked up to the horse Gill had brought forth: Ain't this Hurry's bit?

Gill patted the horse: Yes'r.

Where is he? asked Hoover Pickens.

Weak.

Hoover Pickens looked at Adam: he remembered the morning he had sent him to pick up the contents of Curtis Willow's pocket, how he had handed him the envelope, how weak he was. This was Adam's killing.

Now he—Hoover Pickens—would be the grandfather leading the genetic line up the stairs of his own house, a photo of him in white, and Adam and Adam's sons, until the genetic line traveled upward, up to the round and full belly of the moon until the milk, like castration, spewed out and drowned the world.

He remembered, too, how the Bullocks had laughed at him, Weak? they asked, Weak?, as if to mock the symptoms of his dull-bladed syringe—a shot, a gland he could neither aim nor hold and be one man at one time—or any or all of what he produced, Adam could, too, be this . . . courageous.

He would show them, prove to the other free and automatic men that he belonged to this world and the one following, that he belonged to . . . and now, at such a time, must he show it? he thought.

Yes, he answered, now, as good a time as any. Something good's done come and it's mine and his, Adam's, and belongs to us. As good a time as any.

Adam looked upon his father. He was fully suited, his eyes shone through the pale fabric. He had been silent until now. His father could not see it, nor anyone else in the world: he had begun to weep through the white. They had mastered a discrepancy within him, molded him—like dirt and clay—into a murderer.

Ya! Ya! he yelled, causing Blade to strike out, gallop in the direction of the Thomas house, Gill and his father behind him.

They had reached the Thomas house now, Adam in front.

His father reared up beside him and Gill, the third person, lay in wait behind them, watching the porch-lit globe of the lantern sputter and turn from the base of the wick.

Son, said Hoover Pickens, turning to Adam.

Adam, upon his instruction, trotted toward the steps of the porch and yelled: Nigger, come out yonder.

A long pause, a long wait, and nothing, nothing opened or came to. They could hear only the distant, wailing sound of Midnight, woken with sleep from Adam's bed, ricocheting through the trees.

Adam reared his horse, and Blade, one hoof in front, came down upon the earth with a crashing blow. Suddenly, ill-methodically, the door opened.

Emma New stepped forward: Been wait'n, she uttered.

She looked down at the lantern, barefoot and gowned, and disappeared into the mouth of the house. What had she done? Stumbled? Fainted? For they heard a disturbing noise in the body of the room, the sound of surrender: she dragged the body out of the house. It was fully wrapped in gauze, she took it up beneath the arms and it moved a little, moaned, the head resting on the edge of the porch, as if she positioned it in such a way to love it as if it were dead.

Gill stepped down from his saddle and pushed Emma New aside: he picked up the lantern, sent it crashing through the horizontal window, and set the entire house ablaze, pulling the body near the pulley that had been attached to Blade.

Hoover Pickens stood on the earth now, Adam watching, and walked over to Emma New—her hands were drawn together, as Sonny's had been, and her back was away from the happening—when he reached her, he beckoned for her to face him: Turn around, nigger, he yelled.

Indeed, she turned, the house burning.

Smart nigger, ain't ya? he said, pointing to the gauze, the moaning body. That won't stop 'm from hurtin' none.

He had drawn an invisible line across her face, it quivered in the starkness of her cheek, fluttered throughout her bones like a hummingbird, systematic and disproportionate in width to the character of her standing.

Hitch 'm up, son, he urged.

Adam had not weakened, but carried the demand in his stomach: Gill accompanying him, he looked at the shoe of the gauzed man, felt his resistance, and gathered the sound of Midnight stirring from his sleep with that of the shot that struck his leg out from under him.

No one had ever looked, considered the risk a boy takes to breathe.

His father had traveled away from Emma New and looked down upon the hitched nigger and kicked him in the ribs, until his foot felt the blow, he had cracked a bone.

He halted a moment: a peculiar setting of the thing he had done. And wondered why, with such narcissism within him, was he under the intimate, familiar scope of something horrible, the jungle blood, perhaps, the possibility of belonging to this animal, this creature . . . what bone was he a part of? Certainly not his. Certainly not . . . a nigger's?

The thought of it plagued him and he grew more imperfect, more solidified, as when he had kicked the nigger before, and he dug for the loose rib with his foot and felt it floating in the nigger's stomach and pushed, pushed, until the moaning was unbearable.

Emma New yelled out in the distance, Go, take 'm.

Hoover Pickens spat on the ground in front of her and was proud . . . his boy had taken it, made it this far, and was not weak or sick at the stomach . . . and he urged them, Adam and Gill, to get on their horses and they, they dragged him, the nigger hollered out and they dragged him, the ground burning the gauze, burning his vertebrae into grit.

Hoover Pickens yelled out: Take 'm to the wheelbarrow!

And Adam, the hooded Klan suit suffocating him, steered Blade in the direction of the wheelbarrow and the moon was hot, the moon and the earth and the thing he was a part of suffocated him in his breathing and he took the hood and swung it in the trees and he could breathe now and this was when the load grew lighter—the nigger was dead, had stopped his moaning and lost something, his mouth swung open by the ground, perhaps, his lower mandible beaten and detached at the jawline, a shoe.

Altogether, they needed no light.

They knew the woods, were raised here in the illumination of darkness, only the moon to guide them to the center where the Mississippi leaked into the earth and dust.

Adam halted: the wheelbarrow was yet propped against the tree in the woods, and when he deserted his horse, Gill and his father joined him. He searched with his fingertips for the reins of the pulley and released the feet, one at a time, from the restraints.

The nigger had not lost a shoe, but something else: an eye.

Hoover Pickens stood next to Adam. When the feet were taken out of the pulley, he knelt beside the corpse, the gauze had ripped clear to the bones, and he felt it, the sweltering heat of the grit on the spinal column, the nigger was dead.

Good boy, Adam.

Gill could not see Adam's expression, but he sensed the disturbing horror of his volition. Whatever it was, he had killed it. Adam had killed it and had come to and Gill heard the discomfort of his voice when he answered his father: Grace.

Hoover Pickens took to his horse, trotted homeward and away from the corpse, the web of his impatience spun around him the bloody stain of a birthmark.

chapter
twenty-nine

A bird came down, flew, and arched its turning head in front of him—up there, the sky protruding and swollen about the face, as if it had roamed all night like this, as if the debilitating luster of the living world had made it that way.

The bird suspended, batted its eye, and measured the prediction and substance of Hoover Pickens's posture: his hand wavered ahead, as if to disassociate himself from the looming of the bird: the creature flew and paused, paused with inclination, and would not leave him be.

He looked up at the window, Adam sleeping, and stepped into the wood.

The bird, its beak ajar, trailed him, hung closely to the oxygen, the revelatory symptoms of the morning, and nipped him: Hoover Pickens swung at it, his fists upward and spurring, but the bird would not release him and nipped him again . . . near the throat.

Hoover Pickens struck out, the flesh of his larynx and earlobe bleeding, struck out and ran toward the wheelbarrow in an effort to see what he had done.

The bird called out, like Sonny, and chased him through the forest, nipping him, nipping until its wing shifted with agility, full-blown, and weaved and darted ahead, above the wheelbarrow where Hoover Pickens had fallen to his knees: the bloated head, the eye loosed, hung in the wheelbarrow, and he saw that it was Hurry whose rib he had kicked out of position; he saw, too, the burned vertebrae. The rigor mortis had singed it, swollen and odorous.

He could not stick his foot in the belly now, could not shake the rib, when it seemed so apparent that the killing was not Adam's but his—his own rib and lung suffocating.

There, dangling from the edge of the corpse's pocket, was an envelope, dotted and folded. He reached for it: *To the Men of the Pauer Plant. Courtesy of the Pastor*; it told and warned, each of the symptoms striking him intimately, of an invisible, needle-like pang in the lungs, a bloody cough, the body shutting down, and the final warning, the Pauer Plant of Bullock, Mississippi.

He could not take it all down, the memory of Earl Thomas, the morning he'd pinned him down at the factory, spat in his face, the laughter—how they had mocked him collectively—ape, they had called him. Ape.

Earl Thomas had simply come to save them.

Hoover Pickens turned from the rotted corpse and vomited.

Just now he saw it: beneath the eye of the wheelbarrow lay the name of Hurry Bullock written upon the boarded cross Sonny had made.

And so, in his quest, he followed the stench of rigor mortis through the forest, to where the shot had been fired: Lenora Bullock, dead in her costume jewelry, lay frozen and dead, the little bit of brain that oozed out on her shoulder now a massive heap of flesh. It had pushed her shoulder downward, her waist and hips fat like the pregnant stain of a whistle.

epilogue

Midnight, soon the train will come.

Where was Gill? Adam?

Sonny Willow and the Thomases sat in the waiting area of the train station: now that they had gotten over, the fear of their waiting pounded into their constructive mannerisms a vein of abominable restlessness.

They were accompanied by the accordion player and the mother of the nude child—she was linear in her sitting, wilted and dangling from her chair like the indeterminable resistance of a pansy; her hair had been bathed in the Mississippi this evening, out behind the train station: she brought it over her shoulder, wrung it out, and the nude child was not there but in Memphis with a woman and her husband, for she had seen the doctor and retrieved to her purse the medicine, but it was addictive, like hypocrisy; she was not so vile, she thought. She was not so morose and unkind that she could not hold on. To what? she thought. Dignity?

The accordion player touched her shoulder, not really her shoulder, but the hair she had bathed in the Mississippi: of course, he had seen her near the water's edge, her head churning in the direction of the stream, had seen her dip her face and hair in the

235

Mississippi and come up singularly, alone, patting her hands together.

He would have asked, had his voice not been crushed by the cog wheel, How did you get here? Come so far?, but he could not ask, not ever, when she seemed so random, promiscuous as to leave him standing, watching her without any regret, a ruse.

Now that you've got it, you've given it away? Chosen to lose it? he wanted to ask, for she had been waddling in her purse, the coupons mounding, and stuck her finger to the hollow and lopsided pocket of the rib of the thing she carried and emerged with powder, rouge, a bone-colored tube of lipstick.

And when she arranged her face, she looked to him like confetti: shaped and vertical, blown out of proportion and glaring about.

She stood from her chair and walked toward the horizontal window; the room could be seen in her reflection, Sonny and the Thomases—relics of where she once sat and stood, waited—how they flinched in the room, the sound of wind pushing the doorbell into a murmur. They looked upon her without judgment, never minding the powder, the rouge, the bone-colored lipstick. And with this, she chuckled within: her lips ajar, the purse dropped from her tiny hand.

The coupons had fallen out.

Sonny knelt to protect the contents of her privacy: the mother of the nude child joined her, looked up at the Thomases, and, with intimacy, remarked upon the coupons, Yes, the doctor. Memphis, and pushed them forward and grabbed hold for a moment of Sonny's quivering hand.

Neither she nor the Thomases were in need of the vouchers, but this gesture, separate and apart from the cruel symmetry of the world, hovered unanimously over her and the mother of the nude child; they were unseparate, unapart of the constitution.

They were no longer included, willed out of the Garden at once, out of Bullock and into the aboriginal liturgy of the condition they had been born into: Sonny took up the vouchers, the mother of the nude child facing the poise of the horizontal window, as if what she was now was the moment she had always been and nothing could smear her cheek, rip the line from her face.

It was hers, nothing to blur.

Sonny had returned to her chair when Earl Thomas began to think: where was Gill? Adam? He had not seen them since they brought him here, Emma New here and Sonny and the light of the room, so dim it was, that he could not alter the perplexity of his position; he sat, holding Emma New in his head, shaping her from the outer; it was he who wanted to be held. Right now he wanted her to take him inward, bring her into her bosom and draw him together.

But he was invisible, unseen and without purpose, in this place. And when he thought, in this place, the place he equated in his mind and body was the town of Bullock and, too, the church . . . no one had seen him, no one had crept into his rib and bone, the visceral aptitude of his reaching out, steadying himself on the base of a drum, pounding and pounding in his discomfort the startling effects of the word. Of *nigger*.

How he hoped now that he would never have to hear it, that it would explode, collide with the elements of earth and sky, fire and never belong; he looked at Emma New, the smut of the burning house on her blouse, and wanted her to touch him, at this juncture, so the predicament of what brought them together could let him go.

But Emma New did not hold him: the accordion player held her attention. Why had he looked to her so perturbed, so fidgety? He had not at all spoken, his hand drawn to the fabric of his collar.

He was still, upright, and had woken in the room with a con-founded gaze about him. In her restlessness, she had stripped him of his lung-wind, like Eucharist, opened his mouth and fertilized him, driven him into the ground.

The door of the train station was ajar: the accordion seller's face was turned to the railing. He had not fully come in; he stood unan-nounced, the irrigation of age settling into the contours of his hip.

Are you sour? the obese woman would ask each morning, her lips puckered with conservation, as if she had returned upon him the silly, unapproachable comment he had made in his head at the sight of her: Too fat. Of course, she was aware of the language, the obligatory diction a man held and hooked above her. She had followed him home to the outskirts of Bullock, nipped and nipped like a fat, blistering bird at his bones, the religious and unkind slurs he had mocked, pounded into her head that she was of no use to a man like him, no use to anything worthy of vision.

She bore a pouch within her, unlike the pregnant weight of the child, and she had pulled it out, plucked and plucked, until the hip bone, the thigh, eroded and, too, his constant and erosive commenting, plucked until he could no longer manipulate, de-struct the orphanage with the symptoms of his blotted and dis-torted line.

She had seen the accordion player, how he wrote down the terms of interrogation: *Old one dead. Have mercy.* But she had kept it, clayed and confined like the majestic intimacy of her sandal-toed foot: long before he had carried her home, she had taken his power.

And so the door opened fully and the accordion seller emerged carrying an instrument, nodding to Sonny and the Thomases, the mother of the nude child who stood at the horizontal window, the fog of her breath, the Mississippi, circulating throughout.

The accordion player stood erect from his chair, taking the

bound journal from his pocket, jotting down in more definitive terms, the word: *Mercy?*

Whether it was the shape of the thing he had written or the pitiful, elusive trap the accordion seller had been reduced to was unknown: the accordion seller looked around him, at Sonny—she had begun to pat her knee—and the seat beside her and all the rows of the train station, the bodies they possessed, how naked and dirty they were, and down at the instrument and the jotted line and, conclusively, at his crumbling hip where the obese woman had nipped him and handed over the accordion.

Had he been asked this morning, if this hour was suitable and fit for him, the accordion player would have dreamed less of them, less of the hours and the time it took to wait, for so long a time, to have pleasure and be pleased by another person born miraculously—everything, even the accordion seller, was miraculous now—to him, to give and add, to replenish the thing he had lost and tumbled.

Certainly, the tumbling was his fault, he thought. He should have been more astute, more timely with his tunes, possessive of the instrument, the only sound in the world.

He lifted the accordion, tested a note, and placed the instrument on the seat from which he had begged, slept, picking up the bound journal, but the jotted line was strictly his and that of the man who mercied him.

The accordion seller nodded.

The doorbell rang again.

The accordion player had left the waiting area, vanishing altogether.

Now Adam stood before Sonny Willow.

He had come out of the woods, he and Gill, with the scent of running horses, soot.

Gill was at the ticket counter, Memphis, Tennessee, he said, and when they heard it—the mother of the nude child, the Thomases, and the accordion seller who had become an axis of growth and abandonment—looked at one another, each looking and glaring about, as if the news were an ill-adjustment to the outcome, the thing that had suddenly propelled them into a matter they could not hold.

Adam had come through, approached Sonny Willow and asked her to come here, Follow me, and she had moved her shoulder, stood from her chair, and followed him to the edge of the Mississippi, out behind the train station, where the mother of the nude child's hair had been doused and wet, and said to her: Even when I said it in my head . . . Sonny hushed him and turned to the whistling, pregnant train, the light seeping through the wooded forest and brought her hand inward, to the fabric of her blouse.

As equally as her vocabulary, he, too, stood in the Garden, naked and without, and said to her, You are the woman and you are in it, and now take this part and eat of it and whatever it was that ground you into powder, it is ours and belongs to us: for at this moment she knew that she was the woman: she had taken it up, the mercy, and now that it was so powerful, stood above her rib and bone, she knew that she was chosen, that she could hold her lung-wind and yet breathe and be hers.

It was in her belly that Adam stood.

Adam dug into his pocket, retrieving the envelope Gill had stolen from his father's barn, and handed it to Sonny: he had clung to the envelope, all this time clinging to it, ever since Emma New shared with him how she'd found Midnight, how frail and sick he was from the bullet, ever since he spat in Hurry Bullock's face.

And so it was written: *For Sonny.*

The envelope, the whistling train, went down Sonny's throat and she could only behold the final contents with the seamless, unwavering devastation of a remote and viable constitution . . . she had loved Curtis as though he were dead, even in her waiting near the window, even when she swallowed, and he knew it.

Perhaps she would never open it, she thought, she could take it down, into her belly where the other matters of the world grew naked, anthropologic, down into the dust of waiting.

It could be any of the things she had learned to live without.

She tucked the envelope in her blouse, knelt beside the edge of the Mississippi, and stuck her face in the waters of which Curtis Willow had bathed: of course, this was where he had been, the river had spun a web around him, had drawn and bound him, the poison rushing through.

Wherever he was, he was in one piece, altogether one with dust and earth, and now that her face was in it, she uttered some phrase, beneath the waters, something belonging to her and Curtis alone, her oxygen bellowed out from the Mississippi and drifted on the bed of the current, up toward the exaltation of the lighted moon. The river seeped through her parted mouth and she swallowed and knew that she was swallowing the grit of his vertebrae, his rib.

Gill joined Adam at the edge of the Mississippi: It's time, he said.

The Thomases, the mother of the nude child, the accordion seller were all waiting to board the train. The Negro porter stood at the loading dock, he had come from behind the ticket counter and looked at Sonny, who was now in line, at the Thomases and the horizontal window of the waiting room: the boy who had touched him stood there.

If anyone, anyone had ever touched him like that, he could not pinpoint, say in his mind, who they were or mock with his eye the matter by which they had done it: but yes, a bird had woken him from a dream, flown down beside him—he could no longer remember where, up north, maybe—landed on the branch of his arm without restriction and the yelling, the niggers, the train talk let him go: the umbilical heat of dust and cloud had flung him out of it, the morbidity of two things, two reflections . . . he had not been the catalyst, had not introduced either of the two happenings, and now, as he looked at the boy who had touched him, he eased his hand from the railing, away from the horizontal window, and walked toward the boarding line.

The conductor stepped forward, took the mother of the nude child's coupon, and, with expression, signaled to her how dirty she was: her wrist was outstretched. She wanted him to take it, to help her onto the train, but he looked at her as if to remark, That's what you get, and busied himself with the accordion seller, whose fragility led him to abandon the train, people, and their audacities: the whirring of the machine, how the conductor reached out to him—he was at once muted, his lips mobile and ruse-like, a trick—he let go of the ticket, spawned and returning to the distance.

The Negro porter stood beside the conductor: Sonny, her face smeared from the waters of the Mississippi, approached the conductor, Emma New behind her; the conductor, a superlative nature about him, took up their tickets and pointed to their seating area.

Sonny ahead of her, Emma New was led down the aisle of the train by another Negro porter: his fingers were spread apart and he announced their coming to the others, those who waited and breathed near the closed window—they would have to share the district of air, the circulatory oxygen dispersing through the singular vent—in their exhalation, each shifted farther, more exclamatory in her sleep: with specificity, they paused and moaned equally, one wind, one discomfort, arriving simultaneously on the same nuclear pulse.

A woman, roused from her sleep with interruption, stared at Sonny, Emma New, through the moonlit space around her; someone, these two people, had been seated here, excavated and stirring with whispers: they had come to take up her air, she thought, her wind, with their whispers, their unsympathetic panting, their scattering about.

She sat erectly from her seat, looked out at the other sleepers, those who had come this far with a gratefulness about them. Didn't they, the two women, know of the air they breathed? she thought. One line and hum? One muscle?

Emma New's foot had begun to pat, the patting of it chilled her, the suddenly off-kilter tune that seemed without obligation to the climate of her ill-adjustment.

And she would just keep on patting her foot like that with no music, no keys, nothing to bring her out of it, thought the woman. She leaned forward and clipped her thumb and index fingers together in the pattern of shears, and signaled for the two women, the interrupters, to be quiet now and until she and the other sleepers reached Memphis, until the oxygen in this cart could break, be free.

Emma New's patting had come to a halt. No music, no keys, only the hesitation, the cartilage in her bones burning. What if he don't make it? she thought. What if Earl can't get through? Her weight shifted with interrogation toward Sonny, but Sonny could not answer her now: she, too, was a part of the silent, whirring room, the envelope in her bosom rising without pattern through her blouse and full heart.

With no response to compare her shifting against, Emma New's isolation had become a part of the line and hum, the circulatory breathing of the sleepers. She thought inwardly that the woman should have kept on clipping, clipped and clipped until she no longer would have to think of Earl not getting through, until she drew a line down the center of her waiting, exposing the burning bones.

But then, for a moment of longevity, she thought of her own selfishness, Curtis Willow in the wheelbarrow, how they'd kicked him, beaten him, the worm crawling out.

Her head spun in her seating.

She was remote, unapart of the invisible tune, the key. She was as naked and bare as the shifting, the patting of her foot, and could not interpret fully her isolation; so bold and sparring it was in her mind—the images, Earl's not yet coming through—that she with-held her breath from the sleepers, Sonny and the waiting, as if anyone would notice.

The woman who had done her clipping rose from her seat, the room filled with dark, suffocating people, and brought her index and thumb finger up to Emma New's nostril, and clipped, clipped, as if to say, We don't care, and returned to her slumber.

Earl Thomas had given his ticket to the conductor: he looked down at his feet and up, up to the Negro porter, thinking singu-larly, Now you, too, must, a single stitch binding them collectively to the invisible fabric of servitude.

The Negro porter, yet a part of the morbidity of two things, two reflections stared into the horizontal window, into the eyes of the boy who had touched him, at the conductor—this was the voice that frightened the bird—he spoke: New help, sir.

An order had come, new help, up north, passed along from the hands of the Negro porter to those of the conductor, delivered and brought forth with the irrevocable quality of privilege: with this, the conductor held the ticket, signaled for Earl Thomas to board the train, the redemptive symmetry of rib and bone lingering throughout.

Earl Thomas took his seat beside Emma New, whose hand was now up to the window, her palm pressed in the direction of Adam, Gill, in the distance: Sonny, the Thomases, each sitting near the window, peered at them, the thing they had done, upright and rooted from the gritty vertebrae of a corpse.

Adam turned, the train whistle blowing, as if an inexplicable, elusive thread were tied and drifted from his fingertip: he motioned upward to the bleeding moon, now that he had held it—the invisible kite, the bird—he could let it go.

There, blanketed by the earth, Gill watched, as the invisible kite floated upward, away from the thread of Adam's immobility, up there with no bullet to evoke upon its drifting an irredeemable moaning of the bone.

The train whistled a second time.

The horses began to stir: now Gill was near the side of the train station, holding the reins. Blade reared and paused, reared with the company of the remaining horse. After the third whistle, the train disappearing, Gill settled Blade and released the reins of the second horse, sending it running throughout the suffocating womb of the wooded forest.

Gill looked out at Adam, how well he stood, saying alone, We have whispered, one to another, and won: not only had he held this, but the place he would go, wherever it was, it awaited him, and he would go with this blood and bone and wake in the morning with nothing stirring around him, only his isolation, the remarkable silence of breathing to consider.

He had begun to howl.

With this, he kicked Blade in the ribs, darting out, vanishing under the bleeding moon, until at once he was a part of the transparent, invisible thread.

Adam stood in the dust: he was drawn to it, the place of which he had fallen upon hearing the news, the shot that had taken Midnight's leg out from under him: the consumptive attachment, the shape of catastrophe, drew him closer, and with his bare foot, he shifted the earth as his father had the rib of the dead.

He was extraordinary, nude.

Now that he had come into the world, he stood in his coming of age an announcement to the constitution of the men who'd deemed him the naked proprietor of a killing in this town.